全民英檢初級

口說測驗

曾利娟◎著

晨星出版

Melody 的神奇教學

外籍老師的推薦　Lester Preston

Lester Preston 簡介：

Lester Preston has lived in Taiwan and China for the past eleven years before recently moving back to the United States where he now resides in California. He taught English for two of those years in a variety of schools, cram schools, as well as private lessons. He also taught students to prepare for the oral section of the GEPT test. Lester enjoys studying Chinese, traveling to other countries, and lifting weights.

　　Lester Preston 回美國之前，在台灣和大陸共居住了 11 年，現則居住加州。他過去有兩年的時間任教於各個學校及補習班，同時也擔任家教，教導學生準備全民英檢的口說測驗。Lester 喜歡學習中文，到不同國家旅行以及舉重。

I worked with Melody while I was teaching English in Taiwan, teaching students to prepare for the GEPT among other things. She has been analyzing a lot of teaching material and doing research on GEPT tests. She is a very experienced teacher and enthusiastic about teaching English. Students she taught always spoke highly of her. She helps a large number of students pass the tests and get licenses. The book includes her creative methods and practical tips. I have stayed in China and Taiwan for 11 years. For Chinese, there are some difficulties in learning English, which differ from other nationalities. This book has been specifically designed for Chinese-speaking students. It is not only the best tool for Taiwanese to pass the GEPT, but it is also very useful in oral communication. Don't miss it.

　　我在台灣時，和Melody老師一起教導學生如何準備全民英檢考試，她一直不斷地分析及研究很多的英文教材及全民英檢的測驗題型。她是一位教學經驗十分豐富的老師，並且對教學充滿了熱誠。她所教過的學生都對她讚佩不已，她幫助了很多學生通過測驗並且獲得到證書。這本書包含了她的創意英文學習法以及許多實用的秘訣。我在大陸和台灣待了11年，了解到對華人而說，學習英文有一些和其他國家的人不同的困難之處，而這本書就是特別為說中文的學生所設計的，它不只是台灣學生要通過全民英檢最棒的工具書，對於英語的溝通會話練習也同樣有非常大的幫助。別錯過了這本好書喔！

Melody 的神奇教學

外籍老師的推薦　Tim Watson

Tim Watson 簡介：

Tim Watson started teaching EFL in Asia in 1986. He has taught in Taiwanese university, college, and high school. He has his master's degree and has publications through TESOL.

提姆華生從 1986 年開始在亞洲教英文，曾經任教於台灣的大學、專科和高中。他擁有英語碩士的學位，並著作有英語教學的書籍。

I think this book should be a huge help for students preparing for the oral test of GEPT (General English Proficiency Test). I don't know of any better study guides. Once you have been trained by these books, you will be ready for the test.

我認為這本書對於正在準備全民英檢口說測驗的學生來說，幫助是非常大的。我不知道有其他比這本書更好的學習指引。一但你受過本書的訓練，你就有足夠的能力準備去參加考試了。

Melody 老師的神奇教學

陳柔欣同學推薦

今年我能以基測 286 分接近滿分的成績進入了台中女中，這都要歸功於 Melody 老師的神奇教學。想當初我在國一要參加英檢時因考試經驗不是很豐富，而初試與複試相隔的時間又非常短促的情況下，參加英檢我深怕會準備不足而擔心怯步，但在 Melody 老師完整的重點整理、教導並且鼓勵之下，讓我在最短的時間內，就熟悉了口說的考題規則與答題技巧。因此在考試時，我便能立刻進入狀況，一聽到題目就能了解而立即作答，絲毫沒有因為是第一次參加英文口試而緊張，並以「滿分」的成績通過英檢！真的很感謝 Melody 老師對我的教導。

聽說老師要出書，我非常的高興，希望老師的書能大賣，也希望有更多的人跟我一樣在老師的教導之下以聽力、閱讀及口說皆「滿分」的成績通過英檢。

陳韻如同學推薦

我現在就讀弘文中學，國中一年級就通過全民英檢的測試，而且第二關的口試還考到 100 分（滿分哦！）。一拿到成績單，我就去找 Melody 老師，告訴她我很感謝她。因我是一個非常不喜歡刻板教育的學生，尤其是「文科」！一大束西要背的，想來就頭量。但在上過 Melody 老師的課之後，對於英文要「死背」的印象就徹底改觀，反而還愛上了學習英文。

Melody 神奇的教學技巧，竟能如此準確掌握住考試的重點，「猜題」超準的，在考前所上的課中竟都有準備到。我問她為什麼竟然可以知道考試的內容，她告訴我考試是有所謂的「信度」與「效度」的吻合。雖然我依然不清楚那是什麼，只知道在考前 Melody 老師就已預測我會高分通過，我想這和 Melody 老師深厚的教學能力有所關連吧。

只要體驗過 Melody 老師的教學，你就能了解我所說的這神奇的轉變。不相信？看完這本書後，相信你也會有所改觀，會因而喜歡上英文，所以通過英檢也就是件理所當然的事。

作者序

口說測驗準備方向大解析

By Melody

第一部份準備方向：

　　第一部份爲複誦，所以模仿是很重要的，錄音播出時，要仔細聽句子的語氣及語調，試著儘量去模仿，養成平時模仿標準音調的習慣。例如：句子會因在肯定句、問句或驚嘆句等不同的狀況下，語調就有所不同。

1　　肯定句：She is going to get married.
　　　問句：Is she going to get married?
　　　　　（將 is 放在句首爲問句，語調提高）
　　　驚嘆句：She is going to get married!

　　考生會好奇，爲什麼會有複誦這一大題。這讓我想起美國語言學家所研究的一個案例：美國有一個社工人員發現一個13歲的小女孩，耳朵的聽力正常、智商正常。可因父親是精神病患，只容許她看電視不准她開口說話，雖然她看了近10年的電視，但她仍然不會說話。在訓練了很久後，小女孩好不容易會開口說她最愛的牛奶 "milk"，可沒想到在她極度飢餓的狀況下，還是必須在看到牛奶時，才會說出 "milk"。可見學習語言一定要開口說，不能只聽不說。

　　作者再與讀者分享另一個光聽不說，以致學習效果有限的實例：我這幾年由於教學因素，導致聲帶受損而無法唱歌。所以在教會裡唱英文詩歌的時候，我只能聽和開口 follow up（跟著和），而無法發出聲音唱出歌詞來，所以縱使這些歌曲我已經聽了多次，但就是無法記下歌詞。相反地，七、八年前我在美國時，學會許多英文詩歌，因為那時不用教書，我都是大聲唱出歌詞來的，而至今都仍未忘詞。由此可知，學習英語是否有開口模仿可是非常重要的。

　　第一部份準備方向，重點在於發出聲音、試著去模仿。請考生不要因為在學校是群體上課，就馬虎應付，只有嘴巴跟著張開，而不發出聲音 "read out"（讀出聲音），這樣在學習說英文的效果上可是會大打折扣的。

第二部份準備方向：

　　第二部份是朗讀句子和短文，考生需注意視覺上容易混淆的字。有些功能字--英文稱作 function word，像介詞、 be 動詞及 and 等，輕讀即可，不需要重讀；有些字是關鍵字則需重讀。本書當中的五次模考，我們附上數字圈圈，讓讀者瞭解需重讀或輕讀的部份。圈圈的數字愈大表示讀音愈重，圈圈的數字愈小表示讀音愈輕。第二部份考生亦可以自行錄音，再比較自己與 CD 中的正確發音，讓自己更清楚明白自己的發音及語調，以利糾正自身缺點。

常考補充：
A 類：容易混淆的字群 1
　　　1. talk（說）／ take（拿，花費，搭乘）
　　　2. walk（走）／ wake（醒來）
　　　3. went（go 的過去式）／ won't ＝ will not（將不）／ want（想要）

B 類：＋ ed 字尾的發音 ①

　　1. 無聲字尾＋ <u>ed</u> 唸〔t〕，例如：book<u>ed</u>（預定）、watch<u>ed</u>（看）、wash<u>ed</u>（洗）

　　2. 有聲字尾＋ ed 唸〔d〕，例如：lov<u>ed</u>（愛）

　　3. 字尾 $\left\{ \begin{array}{l} \underline{ted} \\ \underline{ded} \end{array} \right.$ 唸成〔ɪd〕，例如：hat<u>ed</u>（恨）、want<u>ed</u>（要）、start<u>ed</u>（開始）、wait<u>ed</u>（等候）need<u>ed</u>（需要）

※本書另附有考試中心指定必考的單字（請參考後面附錄表）

C、 在第二部份朗讀句子和短文的時候，不能太慢或太快，也不要在不該停頓的地方停頓。

　　例如：There is △ too much traffic △ in big cities.

　　此句若無法一氣呵成，就只能在△處作呼吸換氣。

　　千萬別唸成 There △ is too △ much traffic in △ big cities.

　　那就會聽起來很怪，且讓聽的人不容易了解其意義。

第三部份的準備方向 ①

　　大部分考生都覺得英檢口說的第三部份是最困難的，因為它著重的不只是在口說而已，還必須聽得懂問題的意思，且要能夠在極短的時間內立即想出如何回答問題。因此在這個部份英文聽力佔了很重要的部份，而這對考生來說也是個很大的挑戰。對大多部份的學生而言，是能否通過英檢口說的關鍵就在於第三部份。

　　所以在這一個單元裡，作者用十大句型來幫助考生歸納出最有可能出現的題型，加上關鍵字(key word)還以特別色來標示。讓考生在尚未真正進入模考練習單元之前，就可先訓練自己捉住問題的關鍵字，才能聽得懂問題的涵意，進而回答出適當的句子。

各問題都附有兩句參考的回答例子，因為不是在面談，而是問與答的考試，所以考生可以從兩個例句中找出自己能吸收且能流暢說出的句型，作為將來考試回答問題的來源。亦可以自問自答的方式來訓練自己，以增進英文聽與說的能力。

在這一部份當中，作者以多年的教學經驗及多數考生應考後的經驗分享，扣分最多的情況是答非所問及完全不回答。所以雖然是口說考試，但第三部份的考題是否「聽」得懂問題的意思反而是最基本的得分關鍵。所以本書特別將十大句型之中的題目收錄於CD之中，讓考生可重複訓練聽力。一旦熟悉了各大句型之後，對考生而言，因聽力已進步不少，這時所需注意的只剩下那少數一二個關鍵字，就可完全理解考題。因對你而言，此時句型已不是問題，只要仔細聽好關鍵字，你就已可直接反應了。可還有許多考生，雖然聽得懂問題，卻很怕文法用錯或用詞不當，而錯過回答時間（15秒）。筆者的建議是，大膽回答，儘管文法使用有所錯誤或用詞不是很恰當，但也不至於會完全失去分數，因有回答到關鍵字者，就可得分。例如：What time did you eat dinner last night? 此問題的回答應該要用過去式的吃 'ate' 或 'had' 來表示，若不小心回答 I have dinner at 6 p.m. last night.，就文法上來說 have 不是正確的用法，可是這樣的回答已將關鍵字 '6 p.m. last night' 說出來了，而在這個狀況下分數也不致於被扣掉很多分數的。

目錄
CONTENTS

口說十大句型

句型一至十的題目皆有收錄於 CD 之中

句型一　助動詞為首
先以 yes / no 回答＋Wh 疑問詞的句型

在這一類的句子中，讀者可以重複訓練聽力。在此助動詞反而不是重點，因為這已經成為可以馬上接收的反應了，而真正要去注意的關鍵字僅是特別色的字。

此句型只要以 yes / no 來回答，就有分數可得，例如題目若為 "Do you...?"，就算無法完全聽懂題目，但只要回答 "Yes, I do." 或 "No, I don't." 即有基本分數可得。

因為命題單位了解考生可能會在訓練過後就有回答的基本能力，足以輕鬆應付這類型的問題，所以會在這類型題目的後面增加 why 或 why not 等 wh 的疑問詞，以刺激考生多做回答。

值得注意的是，有時以助動詞為首後接 or 的時候，就不可以 yes / no 回答，否則會變成答非所問。例如 "Do you like noodles or rice better?" 時就不可以用 yes / no 回答。類似這樣的句型是可很簡單作答的，先把 you 改成 I，再從 or 左右各選一項且重複聽力中的句型，答案即可為："I like rice better. / I like noodles better."。

題 1：**Do you exercise? Where do you usually exercise?**
（你運動嗎？你通常都在那做運動？）

答 1：**Yes, I exercise in the gym every other day. I enjoy lifting heavy weights. I usually exercise with some friends. That makes it more enjoyable.**
（是的，我每隔一天會到健身房運動。我喜歡舉重，我通常是跟朋友一起運動，那樣運動起來會更有趣。）

答 2：**Yes, I run 3 kilometers around the field at my school. I do this about three times a week. I'm trying to lose 4 kilograms.**

（是的，我會到學校的運動場跑道跑三公里，每週三次。我現在正試著要減掉四公斤。）

名師解析

- kilograms 可以亦可說成 kilos。
- 也有人可能會回答：
  No, I don't exercise. I am a couch potato!
  （沒有，我不做運動的，我是個成天坐在沙發上看電視的人！）
- couch potato（沙發上的馬鈴薯）指的是一個懶惰不愛運動，成天看電視的人。

題 2：**Do you speak Taiwanese more than Chinese at home?**
（你在家裡說台語比說國語多嗎？）

答 1：**No, we speak Chinese more than Taiwanese at home.**
（不是，我們在家裡說國語比說台語多。）

答 2：**Yes, at home we speak Taiwanese more than Chinese.**
（是的，在家裡我們說台語比說國語多。）

名師解析

- Chinese（中文）可用 Mandarin（北京話）代替，因為全球有 Chinese（華人）的地方，是以 Mandarin（華語／中文）、Cantonese（廣東話）及 Taiwanese（台語）等三種語言最為普遍。

題 3 ： **Do you like to go to movie theaters to see movies or stay at home to watch TV? Why?**

（你喜歡到電影院看電影還是在家中看電視？為什麼？）

答 1 ： **I like to go to movie theaters to watch movies because I like the big screen.**

（我喜歡到電影院看電影，因為我喜歡看大螢幕。）

答 2 ： **I like to stay at home to watch TV because I don't like to be around a lot of people.**

（我喜歡在家裡看電視，因為我不喜歡待在人多的地方。）

名 師 解 析

■ 本題回答必須是 A or B 之中作一個選擇，不可以用 yes / no 回答。

題 4 ： **Do you keep a diary? Why or why not?**

（你有寫日記的習慣嗎？為什麼有或為什麼沒有？）

答 1 ： **I do not keep a diary because I am too tired to do it.**

（我沒有寫日記的習慣，因為太累了所以沒辦法這麼做。）

答 2 ： **I keep a diary because I like to write my experiences and thoughts down on paper.**

（我有寫日記的習慣，因為我喜歡將我的經歷及想法寫在紙上。）

題 5 ： **Do you wake up early? What time do you wake up?**

（你很早起床嗎？你都幾點醒來的？）

答 1： **No, I do not wake up early. I wake up at 9 a.m.**

（不，我不是很早起床的，我都早上九點醒來。）

答 2： **Yes, I wake up early. I wake up at 6 a.m.**

（是，我很早醒來，我都早上六點醒來。）

題 6： **Do you like to live alone or with your parents? Why?**

（你喜歡自己一個人住還是跟父母同住？為什麼？）

答 1： **I like to live alone because I'm independent.**

（我喜歡自己一個住，因為我是很獨立的。）

答 2： **I like to live with my parents because I like my mom to wash my clothes and fix me food.**

（我喜歡和父母同住，因為我喜歡我母親替我洗衣物及準備食物。）

名 師 解 析

- 本題不可以用 yes / no 回答。
- fix 在此與 prepare 同義。

題 7： **Do you have any brothers and sisters? How old are they?**

（你有兄弟姐妹嗎？他們幾歲？）

答 1： **No, I don't. I do not have any brothers and sisters. I am the only child.**

（沒有，我沒有兄弟姐妹，我是獨子／獨生女。）

答 2： **Yes, I do. I have a sister who is 26, another sister who is 22, and a brother who is 17.**

（有，我有一個二十六歲的姐姐，及一個二十二歲的姐姐，還有一個十七歲的弟弟。）

題 8 ： Do you have any pets? If you could have any pet you wanted, what kind of pet would you like to have?

（你有寵物嗎？假如你能擁有任何你想要的寵物，你想要什麼樣的寵物？）

答 1 ： No, I don't. I do not have any pets. If I could have a pet, I'd like to have a dog.

（沒有，我沒有寵物。假如我能擁有一隻寵物的話，我想要一隻狗。）

答 2 ： Yes, I do. I have a pet cat. If I could have any pet I wanted, I would like to have a pony.

（有，我有一隻寵物貓。假如我能擁有任何一種我想要的寵物的話，我想要一匹小馬。）

名 師 解 析

【延伸單字：動物名稱】

fish (n.) 魚	miniature pig (n.) 迷你豬	rabbit (n.) 兔子
turtle (n.) 烏龜	snake (n.) 蛇	bird (n.) 鳥
lizard (n.) 蜥蜴	sheep (n.) 羊	chicken (n.) 雞
horse (n.) 馬	spider (n.) 蜘蛛	squirrel (n.) 松鼠
frog (n.) 青蛙	pony (n.) 小馬；矮種馬	hamster (n.) 倉鼠

題 9 ： Do you like to exercise? Why or why not?

（你喜歡做運動嗎？為什麼或為什麼不？）

答 1： **I like to exercise because I know it is good for my health.**

（我喜歡做運動，因為我知道運動有益我的健康。）

答 2： **I do not like to exercise at all because I don't like to sweat.**

（我根本不喜歡運動，因為我不喜歡流汗。）

名師解析

■ to exercise（運動）可換成其他動詞，如：

to sing（唱歌）　　 to dance（跳舞）

to read（閱讀）　　 to write（寫作）

題 10： **Do you like to eat out or cook at home?**

（你喜歡到外面吃還是在家做飯？）

答 1： **I don't like to cook, so I like to eat out. And I live alone, so eating out is cheaper.**

（因為我不喜歡做飯，所以我喜歡到外面吃。而且我是自己一個人住的，所以到外面吃比較便宜。）

答 2： **I really like to cook, so I lIke to eat at home. Besides, eating out costs more.**

（因為我真的很喜歡做飯，所以我喜歡在家裡吃。除此之外，在外面吃的花費比較多。）

名師解析

■ 本題不可以用 yes / no 回答

題 11 ： **Do you help do housework? If you do, what do you do?**
（你會幫忙做家事嗎？如果有，你做些什麼？）

答 1 ： **No, I don't. All I have to do is study, so I do not help around the house.**
（沒有，因為我都在讀書，所以我不做家事的。）

答 2 ： **Yes, I do. I help my mom wash dishes and I clean my room every week.**
（有，我會幫我媽媽洗碗盤還有每週會打掃我的房間的。）

題 12 ： **Did you lose or gain any weight recently?**
（最近你的體重是減少還是增加？）

答 1 ： **I lost 2 kilos last month because I went on a diet.**
（上個月我減了二公斤，因為我有控制飲食。）

答 2 ： **Recently my weight has stayed the same, although I hope to lose weight.**
（最近我的體重維持不變，雖然我想減重。）

名 師 解 析
■ 本題同是 A or B 的選擇，所以不可以用 yes / no 回答。

題 13 ： **Can you drive a car, and do you drive a car often?**
（你會開車嗎？你常開嗎？）

答 1 ： **Yes, I can. But I seldom drive because I don't have my own car.**
（是的，我會。不過我很少開，因為我沒有自己的車。）

答 2： No, I can't. I am a teenager, and I can't get a driver's license yet.

（不，我不會。我是個青少年，還沒拿到駕照。）

題14： Have you ever traveled by airplane?

（你曾坐飛機去旅行過嗎？）

答 1： Yes, I have. When I went to Hong Kong last year, I traveled by airplane.

（是的。去年我曾搭飛機去香港。）

答 2： Yes, I have. I have traveled by airplane from Taipei to Kaohsiung.

（是的。我曾從台北坐飛機去高雄。）

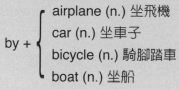

■ by 之後可以換成其他的交通工具，為 by＋交通工具如：

by ＋
- airplane (n.) 坐飛機
- car (n.) 坐車子
- bicycle (n.) 騎腳踏車
- boat (n.) 坐船

而行人走路則用 on foot （徒步）

題15： Can you tell me where I can buy French fries?

（你能告訴我可以在哪裡買到薯條嗎？）

答 1： You can buy French fries at any McDonald's or any other fast food restaurant.

（你可以在隨便一家麥當勞或速食店買到薯條的。）

答 2 ： I'm sorry. I am not familiar with the neighborhood.

（很抱歉，這一帶我不熟。）

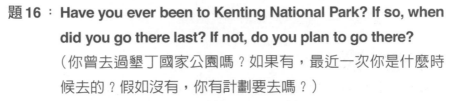

名 師 解 析

■ neighborhood (n.) 鄰近地區
■ buy French fries（買薯條）亦可改成買其他東西如：
newspaper (n.) 報紙
clothes (n.) 衣服
computer (n.) 電腦

題16 ： Have you ever been to Kenting National Park? If so, when did you go there last? If not, do you plan to go there?

（你曾去過墾丁國家公園嗎？如果有，最近一次你是什麼時候去的？假如沒有，你有計劃要去嗎？）

答 1 ： Yes, I have. Last summer my family and I went to Kenting National Park.

（是的。去年夏天，我和我的家人去過墾丁國家公園。）

答 2 ： No, I have never been to Kenting National Park. I hope we can go there next year.

（沒有，我從未去過墾丁國家公園。我希望我們明年能去。）

名 師 解 析

■ Have you ever + Vpp...? 你曾經……？
■ have / has been to... 曾經去過……

題 17 ： **Have you ever cooked for your family?**
（你曾為你的家人做過飯嗎？）

答 1 ： **Yes, I have. I have made breakfast for my family a few times.**
（是的，我有。我曾為我的家人做過幾次早餐。）

答 2 ： **No, I have never cooked for my family.**
（沒有，我沒有。我從未替我家人做過飯。）

題 18 ： **Are you nervous now? What makes you nervous?**
（你現在緊張嗎？什麼事會讓你緊張？）

答 1 ： **No, I am not nervous now, but if I am late for work, it makes me nervous.**
（不，我現在不會緊張。但是如果我上班遲到的話，我會緊張的。）

答 2 ： **Yes, I am nervous now. Speaking English makes me nervous.**
（是的，我現在感到緊張。說英文會讓我緊張的。）

- nervous (a.) 緊張的
  同義字： scared
  afraid
  frightened

題 19 ： **Are there many of your friends taking a test today? If so, how many?**

（今天你有很多朋友過來考試嗎？如果有，有多少人？）

答 1 ： **Yes, four of my friends are taking a test today.**
（有的，我有四位朋友來參加今天的考試。）

答 2 ： **No, none of my friends are taking a test today.**
（沒有，我朋友們今天沒有過來參加考試。）

題20 ： **Do you think your friends like you? Why or why not?**
（你覺得你的朋友喜歡你嗎？為什麼或為什麼不？）

答 1 ： **I think my friends like me because I'm funny.**
（我想我的朋友是喜歡我的，因為我很爆笑。）

答 2 ： **I think my friends like me because I'm easygoing.**
（我想我朋友是喜歡我的，因為我很好相處。）

題21 ： **Do you like to listen to music while you are studying? Why or why not?**
（你讀書時，喜歡聽音樂嗎？為什麼喜歡或為什麼不喜歡？）

答 1 ： **I like to listen to music. It helps me study better.**
（我喜歡聽音樂，它讓我讀書的效果更好。）

答 2 ： **I do not like to listen to music because I can't concentrate on my studies when I listen to music.**
（我不喜歡聽音樂，因為當我聽音樂時，我無法專心學習。）

題22 ： **Do you like to study English? Why or why not?**
（你喜歡學習英文嗎？為什麼或為什麼不？）

答 1 ： **I like to study English because I want to travel abroad.**

（我喜歡學英文，因為我想到國外旅行。）

答 2：I do not like to study English because English grammar is so difficult.

（我不喜歡學英文，因為英文文法很難。）

題 23：Do you like to read the newspaper? Why or why not?

（你喜歡看報紙嗎？為什麼或為什麼不？）

答 1：Yes, I do. I like to read the newspaper because I like to know what is happening in the world.

（是，我喜歡看報紙，因為我想知道世界現在發生什麼事情。）

答 2：No, I don't. I do not like to read the newspaper because I do not have time.

（不，我不喜歡看報紙，因為我沒有時間。）

題 24：Do you go to bed late? What time do you go to bed at night?

（你很晚睡嗎？你晚上都幾點睡覺？）

答 1：Yes, I do. I go to bed at 1 a.m. every night.

（是，我很晚睡，我每晚都凌晨一點鐘睡。）

答 2：No, I don't , because I go to bed right after dinner.

（不，我不會很晚睡，因為我吃完晚餐後就睡了。）

名 師 解 析

■ 很多人會搞混以下這些用法：

sleep late（睡到很晚）≠ go to sleep late（很晚才睡）≠ oversleep（睡過頭）

句型二　What 為首

　　What 為最常見的聽力句型，所以希望你熟悉之後，可以馬上反應吸收，以讓 what 不須列為關鍵字，之後不再需要特別認真去聽它。

題 1 ： **What fruit do you like best?**

　　　（你最喜歡什麼水果？）

答 1 ： **I like watermelons best.**

　　　（我最喜歡西瓜。）

答 2 ： **I like most fruits, especially guavas.**

　　　（大部份的水果我都喜歡，特別是芭樂。）

名 師 解 析

【延伸單字：水果名稱】

banana (n.) 香蕉	apple (n.) 蘋果	grape (n.) 葡萄
grapefruit (n.) 葡萄柚	orange (n.) 柳丁	papaya (n.) 木瓜
pineapple (n.) 鳳梨	lichee (n.) 荔枝	coconut (n.) 椰子
durian (n.) 榴槤	tangerine (n.) 橘子	

■ 動詞片語之後的副詞最高級 the best 的 the 可以省略

　　like / love... (the) best　最喜歡／愛……

題 2 ： **What subject do you dislike most?**

　　　（你最不喜歡那個科目？）

答 1 ： **I dislike math most.**

　　　（我最不喜歡數學。）

答 2 ： **The subject I dislike most is biology.**

（我最不喜歡的科目是生物學。）

【延伸單字：科目名稱】

Chinese (n.) 國文	English (n.) 英文	math (n.) 數學
history (n.) 歷史	chemistry (n.) 化學	physics (n.) 物理
economics (n.) 經濟學	geography (n.) 地理	biology (n.) 生物
sociology (n.) 社會學	psychology (n.) 心理學	medicine (n.) 醫學

P.E.= physical education (n.) 體育

題 3 ： **What did you eat for breakfast this morning?**

（你今天早上早餐吃什麼？）

答 1 ： **I ate a sandwich for breakfast this morning.**

（今天早上的早餐我吃三明治。）

答 2 ： **I had milk and bread for breakfast this morning.**

（今天早上的早餐我是喝牛奶及吃麵包。）

名 師 解 析

■ had 可以表示「吃」或「喝」，但在外國沒有「喝」湯的
表達，所以不可以說 "drink soup"，必須說 "have soup" 或
"eat soup"。

題 4 ： **What time do you usually get up in the morning?**

（你早上通常都幾點起床？）

答 1 ： **I usually get up at 6 a.m.**

（我通常在六點起床。）

答 2 ： **In the morning, I usually get up at 6:30 a.m.**

（早上我通常都在六點三十分起床。）

題 5 ： **What is the day before Wednesday?**

（星期三之前是星期幾？）

答 1 ： **Tuesday is the day before Wednesday.**

（星期二在星期三之前。）

答 2 ： **The day before Wednesday is Tuesday.**

（星期三之前是星期二。）

名師解析

■ the day before...　在某天之前
the day after...　在某天之後

題 6 ： **What month has only twenty-eight or twenty-nine days?**

（那一個月份只有 28 或 29 天？）

答 1 ： **February usually has twenty-eight days.**

（二月通常只有 28 天。）

答 2 ： **The only month that has twenty-eight or twenty-nine days is February.**

（只有 28 或 29 天的月份是二月。）

題 7：What do you spend most of your money on?

（你在什麼東西上面花最多錢？）

答 1：I spend most of my money on clothes.

（我在衣服上所花的錢是最多的。）

答 2：I spend most of my money on books.

（我在書本上所花的錢是最多的。）

名 師 解 析

■ 亦可以問：

What do you spend most of your time on after school or after work?
（你放學後或下班後在什麼事上面花最多時間？）
學生大部份會回答：
I spend most of my time on study.
（我大部份時間都花在課業上。）

題 8：What do people usually do when they go to a library?

（人們通常都去圖書館做什麼？）

答 1：People usually read in a library.

（人們通常去圖書館看書。）

答 2：Most people borrow books from a library.

（大多數的人們都去圖書館借書。）

題 9：What year were you born in?

（你是在那年出生的？）

答 1：I was born in 1985.

（我在 1985 年出生。）

答 2 ： **1990 was the year I was born.**

（1990 是我出生的年份。）

題 10 ： **What do you usually do when you're stuck in traffic?**

（塞車時，你通常會做些什麼？）

答 1 ： **When I'm stuck in traffic, I listen to the radio.**

（當我遇到塞車時，我會聽廣播。）

答 2 ： **I listen to my CD player when I'm stuck in traffic.**

（當我遇到塞車時，我會聽 CD。）

名 師 解 析

■ be stuck in　被阻塞或被困住

　traffic (n.) 交通，交通量

題 11 ： **What is your hobby?**

（你的興趣是什麼？）

答 1 ： **My hobby is collecting stamps.**

（我的興趣是集郵。）

答 2 ： **I have a rock collection and a coin collection.**

（我收集岩石及收藏硬幣。）

題 12 ： **What present do you want to get on your birthday?**

（你生日想要什麼禮物？）

答 1 ： **I want my parents to get me a CD player for my birthday.**

（我想要我父母送我 CD 隨身聽當生日禮物。）

答 2： **For my birthday, I want a new suit.**

（我想要一套新的套裝／西裝來做為我的生日禮物。）

題 13： **What is your favorite season?**

（你最喜歡那個季節？）

答 1： **My favorite season is spring because it isn't too hot or too cold.**

（我最喜歡的季節是春天，因為它不會太熱或太冷。）

答 2： **My favorite season is winter because I hate hot days.**

（我最喜歡的季節是冬天，因為我討厭大熱天。）

題 14： **What is the place you would like to go to the most? Why?**

（你最想去什麼地方？為什麼？）

答 1： **The place I would like to go to the most is Korea because I've never been there.**

（我最想去的地方是韓國，因為我從未去過那裡。）

答 2： **New York is the place I'd like to go to the most because my girlfriend is studying there.**

（紐約是我最想去的地方，因為我女朋友正在那裡讀書。）

名 師 解 析

■ 動詞片語之後的副詞最高級 the most 的 the 可以省略：
would like = want... (the) most　最想要……

題 15 ： **What do you usually do on weekends? Why?**
（週末你通常都做些什麼？為什麼？）

答 1 ： **I usually study on weekends because I want to get good grades.**
（週末我通常在讀書，因為我想得到好成績。）

答 2 ： **I usually hang out with my friends on weekends because I don't have time during the week.**
（週末我通常和朋友泡在一起，因為在平常日子我沒有時間這麼做。）

名 師 解 析

■ hang out　留在某地、閒晃、待在某地

題 16 ： **What's your favorite pastime activity?**
（你最喜歡的消遣活動是什麼？）

答 1 ： **My favorite pastime is playing computer games.**
（我最喜歡的消遣是玩電腦遊戲。）

答 2 ： **Reading novels is my favorite pastime.**
（看小說是我最喜歡的消遣。）

名 師 解 析

■ pastime (n.) 消遣。用來形容有多餘時間時才有機會做的事。

題 17 ： **What day is your busiest day of the week? What do** you need to do?

（星期幾你最忙碌？你需要做些什麼？）

答 1： **My busiest day of the week is Saturday because I have to clean my room and do all my homework.**

（一週裡我最忙的一天是星期六，因為我必需打掃我的房間和做家庭作業。）

答 2： **My busiest day of the week is Wednesday because I have the most classes on Wednesday.**

（一週裡我最忙的一天是星期三，因為星期三我的課最多。）

題 18： **What are you wearing today?**

（你今天穿戴些什麼？）

答 1： **Today I am wearing shorts and a T-shirt.**

（今天我穿短褲及 T 恤。）

答 2： **I am wearing jeans, and a sweater.**

（今天我穿牛仔褲及毛衣。）

■ wear (v.) 穿；戴
casual wear (n.) 休閒服

題 19： **What are some good ways to learn English?**

（學英文有那些好方法？）

答 1： **Speaking to a foreign friend is a good way to learn English.**

（跟外國朋友交談是學英文的一個好方法。）

答 2： **A good way to learn English is practicing singing English songs.**

（練習唱英文歌是學習英文的一個好方法。）

題 20： **What pet would you like to have? Why?**

（你想要有什麼寵物？為什麼？）

答 1： **I would like to have a dog because a dog is man's best friend.**

（我想要有一隻狗，因為狗是人類最好的朋友。）

答 2： **I would like to have goldfish because they don't cause any trouble.**

（我想要金魚，因為他們不會惹麻煩。）

題 21： **What did you do last weekend?**

（上週末你在做什麼？）

答 1： **Last weekend, I went to a basketball game.**

（上週末我去看籃球比賽。）

答 2： **I went to a movie with my boyfriend last weekend.**

（上週末我和我男朋友去看電影。）

題 22： **What sports do you like the best?**

（你最喜歡什麼運動？）

答 1： **I like tennis and baseball the best.**

（我最喜歡網球和棒球。）

答 2 ： **The sports I like the best are basketball and football.**

（我最喜歡的運動是籃球和美式足球。）

【延伸單字：運動名稱】

jumping rope (n.) 跳繩   volleyball (n.) 排球   bowling (n.) 保齡球

badminton (n.) 羽毛球   frisbee (n.) 飛盤   jogging (n.) 慢跑

hiking (n.) 健行   gymnastics (n.) 體操   skiing (n.) 滑雪

mountain-climbing (n.) 爬山

■ football (n.) 美式足球（橄欖形的足球）

soccer (n.) 世界足球賽的足球

■ hiking，中文稱之為「爬山」，指在山區徒步而不是真的攀爬山崖，而 mountain-climbing 也是爬山，但是指的是用手腳一同攀爬的「爬山」。

■ 動詞片語之後的副詞最高級 the best 的 the 可以省略：

like / love... (the) best 最喜歡……

題23 ： **What is the weather like today?**

（今天的天氣如何？）

答 1 ： **The weather is really nice today.**

（今天的天氣真好。）

答 2 ： **It is too hot today.**

（今天很熱。）

■ 本題題目的意思同：How is the weather today?

題 24 ： **What is your favorite subject?**

（你最喜歡那個科目？）

答 1 ： **Math is my favorite subject because I like to work with numbers.**

（數學是我最喜歡的科目，因為我喜歡數字。）

答 2 ： **My favorite subject is history because I like reading stories.**

（我最喜歡的科目是歷史，因為我喜歡讀故事。）

題 25 ： **What is the weather here like in January?**

（這裡一月的天氣如何？）

答 1 ： **The weather is very pleasant here in January.**

（在一月，這裡的天氣是非常舒適怡人的。）

答 2 ： **In January, the weather is very cold.**

（在一月，天氣是非常冷的。）

名師解析

【延伸單字：月份名】

January (n.) 一月	February (n.) 二月	March (n.) 三月
April (n.) 四月	May (n.) 五月	June (n.) 六月
July (n.) 七月	August (n.) 八月	September (n.) 九月
October (n.) 十月	November (n.) 十一月	December (n.) 十二月

題 26 ： **What kind of music do you like best? Why?**

（你最喜歡那種類型的音樂？為什麼？）

答 1： **I like pop music best because all of my friends like it.**
（我最喜歡流行音樂，因為我所有的朋友都喜歡。）

答 2： **I like soft music the best because it makes me relaxed.**
（我較喜歡輕音樂，因為它讓我放鬆。）

【延伸單字：音樂名稱】

classic (n.) 古典　　　jazz (n.) 爵士　　　country (n.) 鄉村

rap (n.) 饒舌　　　　hip-pop (n.) 嬉哈　　　pop music (n.) 流行音樂

■ pop music 為 popular music 的簡稱

■ What kind of... = What type of...　哪種類型的……

■ 動詞片語之後的副詞最高級 the best 的 the 可以省略：

like / love... (the) best　最喜歡……

題27： **What are you going to do tomorrow?**
（你明天要做什麼？）

答 1： **Tomorrow I am going to the bookstore to pick up some books.**
（明天我要去書店買一些書。）

答 2： **I am going to the dentist tomorrow to get my teeth cleaned.**
（明天我要去牙醫診所去洗牙。）

題28： **What kind of movie do you like the most? Why?**
（你最喜歡那種類型的電影？為什麼？）

答 1：**I like comedies the most because I like to laugh.**

（我喜歡喜劇，因為我喜歡笑。）

答 2：**I like to watch adventure movies because I like adventures.**

（我喜歡看冒險電影，因為我喜歡冒險。）

名師解析

【延伸單字：音樂名稱】

action movie (n.) 動作片 　　 horror movie (n.) 恐怖片

romance movie (n.) 文藝愛情片 　 western movie (n.) 西部片

kung fu movie (n.) 功夫片 　　 cartoon movie (n.) 卡通片

musical movie (n.) 歌舞劇 　　 animation (n.) 動畫

science fiction (sci-fi) movie (n.) 科幻片

■ 動詞片語之後的副詞最高級 the most 的 the 可以省略

題 29：**What is your favorite movie? Why?**

（你最愛的電影是那部？為什麼？）

答 1：**My favorite movie is "Lord of the Rings" because it is very exciting.**

（我最愛的電影是《魔戒》，因為它非常刺激。）

答 2：**"The Phantom of the Opera" is my favorite movie because I really like the songs they sing.**

（《歌劇魅影》是我最愛的電影，因我真的很喜歡他們唱的歌。）

名師解析

■ 本題目亦可以問：What is your favorite book?

題30： **What is your family name? How do you spell it?**

（你姓什麼？怎麼拼呢？）

答 1： **My family name is Chen, C-h-e-n.**

（我姓陳，C-h-e-n。）

答 2： **My family name is Huang, H-u-a-n-g.**

（我姓黃，H-u-a-n-g。）

名師解析

■ family name ＝ surname ＝ last name 家族姓氏

■ first name ＝ given name 名字

題31： **What do you usually do on weekends?**

（你在週末時通常會做些什麼？）

答 1： **I usually clean my room on weekends.**

（週末我通常都在打掃我的房間。）

答 2： **On weekends, I usually spend time with my friends.**

（在週末，我通常都是和我朋友一起渡過的。）

句型三　How 為首

題 1：**How and where did you meet your best friend? Tell me about your best friend.**

（你是如何、在哪裡認識你最好的朋友？談談你最好的朋友。）

答 1：**I met my best friend, George, at school when I was in the first grade. He was in my class. He is very friendly and likes to play basketball.**

（我在學校認識我最好的朋友喬治，當時我一年級。他是我的同學，他很友善且喜歡打籃球。）

答 2：**My best friend is Joanne, who is my cousin. I can't remember when I first met her because we grew up together. She is very shy and artistic.**

（我最好的朋友是瓊安，她是我的堂妹。我想不起來我第一次遇到她是在什麼時候，因為我們是一起長大的，她非常靦腆且很有藝術天份。）

題 2：**How are you today?**

（你今天好嗎？）

答 1：**I'm doing great, how are you?**

（我很好，你好嗎？）

答 2：**I'm fine, and you?**

（我很好，你呢？）

亦可回答：　Can't be better! ＝ Couldn't be better

（再好不過了！）

題 3 ： **How is the weather today?**

（今天的天氣如何？）

答 1 ： **It's really hot, isn't it?**

（實在很熱，不是嗎？）

答 2 ： **It's too cold for me.**

（對我而言，很冷。）

名師解析

■ 天氣的問法可用：

① How is the weather?

② What is the weather like?

題 4 ： **How do you keep in touch with your friends far away?**

（你如何與你在遠方的朋友聯絡的？）

答 1 ： **By e-mail and MSN, I keep in touch with my friends far away.**

（我都用 e-mail 與網路即時通與我在遠方的朋友聯絡。）

答 2 ： **I write postcards, greeting cards or letters to faraway friends. Sometimes, I call them, though it costs a lot.**

（我通常都會寫明信片或信給我在遠方的朋友們，有時候我會打電話給他們，雖然打電話很花錢。）

題 5 ： **How do you save money?**

（你如何存錢？）

答 1 ： **By buying cheaper things, I can save some money.**

（我都買較便宜的東西，這樣就能存一些些錢。）

答 2 ： I put part of my income in the bank and get a little interest.

（我把部份的收入存入銀行，然後收些利息。）

題 6 ： How do you go to work or go to school?

（你如何去工作或學校？）

答 1 ： I ride my motor scooter to school every day.

（我每天都騎機車上學。）

答 2 ： I drive my car to work.

（我開車上班。）

名師解析

■ 機車的說法有：

① motor scooter (n.)

② scooter (n.)

③ motorcycle (n.)

④ motorbike (n.)

題 7 ： How have you been lately?

（你最近過得如何？）

答 1 ： I've been great.

（我過得很好。）

答 2 ： Lately I've been sick.

（最近我生病了。）

題 8 ： How do you study English?

（你如何學習英文？）

答 1 ： I study English by reading magazines, listening to English programs and speaking to foreigners.

（我是靠閱讀雜誌、聽英文節目、和外國人交談學習英文。）

答 2 ： I go to cram school to study English.

（我到補習班學英文。）

題 9 ： How did you come here today? Did you come here alone?

（你今天是如何來這裡的？你自己一個人來嗎？）

答 1 ： I came here alone by bus.

（我是自己一個人坐公車來這裡的。）

答 2 ： I drove here with my friend who sat behind me by scooter.

（我跟我朋友騎機車來這裡的，他坐在我後面。）

亦可回答： My parents drove me here today.

（今天我父母開車送我來這裡。）

I rode my bicycle here.

（我騎腳踏車來這裡。）

題10 ： How long have you lived where you are living now?

（你在現在住的地方住多久了？）

答 1 ： I have lived here for 4 years.

（我住在這裡四年了。）

答 2 ： I have lived in this house all of my life.

（我一輩子都住在這間房子。）

題11： **How long have you been studying English?**
（你英文學多久了？）

答 1 ： **I have been studying English for 6 years.**
（我英文已經學六年了。）

答 2 ： **I began studying English in elementary school, so I have studied for 8 years.**
（我從小學開始學英文，所以我學八年了。）

題12： **How much do you weigh?**
（你有多重？／你體重多少？）

答 1 ： **I weigh 50 kilos.**
（我有 50 公斤重。）

答 2 ： **My weight is a secret.**
（我的體重是秘密。）

名師解析

■ 本題題目的意思同： What's your weight?

題13： **How many hours do you usually sleep every day?**
（你每天通常都睡幾個小時？）

答 1 ： **I only sleep about 6 hours because I have so much homework.**
（我大約只睡六小時，因為我有很多家庭作業。）

答 2 ： **I only get about 5 hours of sleep because I love to play computer games.**

（我大約只睡五小時，因為我喜歡玩電腦遊戲。）

題 14 ： How much did your shoes cost that you are wearing now?

（你現在穿的鞋子花了你多少錢？）

答 1 ： **My shoes cost NT $2,000.**

（我鞋子花了新台幣二千元。）

答 2 ： **I don't know because my mother bought them for me.**

（我不知道，因為是我媽媽買給我的。）

名 師 解 析

■ 鞋子是複數為一雙，所以答2用 "them" 代替問題所問的 shoes。

題 15 ： How long does it take you to go to work or go to school?

（你去上班或去上學要多久？）

答 1 ： **It only takes me 5 minutes to get to school.**

（我去上學只花五分鐘。）

答 2 ： **It takes me half an hour to get to work.**

（我去上班要花上半小時。）

名 師 解 析

■ 半小時的說法有： a half hour
= half an hour
= 30 minutes

題 16 ： **How do you usually celebrate your birthday?**
（你通常如何慶祝生日？）

答 1 ： **My parents usually take me out to eat on my birthday. I get to choose the restaurant.**
（我生日時，我爸媽通常會帶我外出用餐。由我選擇餐廳。）

答 2 ： **My mom makes my favorite food on my birthday, and I can invite some of my friends for dinner.**
（我生日時，我媽媽會做我最愛的食物，且我可以邀請我的一些朋友來共進晚餐。）

題 17 ： **How many minutes are there in an hour?**
（一個小時有幾分鐘？）

答 1 ： **There are 60 minutes in an hour.**
（一小時裡有六十分鐘。）

答 2 ： **An hour has 60 minutes.**
（一小時有六十分鐘。）

題 18 ： **How many kinds of things can you name to wear?**
（你可以說出多少種可以穿戴物品的名稱？）

答 1 ： **Blouses, skirts, T shirts, jeans, shorts, shoes, socks, sandals, boots, dresses, suits, slacks, and sweaters.**
（短上衣、裙子、Ｔ恤、牛仔褲、短褲、鞋子、短襪、涼鞋、長靴、洋裝、套裝、寬鬆長褲及毛衣。）

答 2 ： **Shirts, pants, jeans, shorts, suits, ties, shoes, socks, belts, glasses and necklaces.**

（襯衫、長褲、牛仔褲、短褲、套裝、領帶、鞋子、短襪、皮帶、眼鏡及項鍊。）

名師解析

■ wear (v.) 穿、戴、留，這動詞的用法有很多，如：
wear long hair (v.) 留長髮
wear make-up (v.) 化粧
wear a smile (v.) 掛著笑容

題 19 ： How much time do you spend on the telephone every day?
（你每天花多少時間講電話？）

答 1 ： I spend about an hour on the phone every day.
（我每天約花一個小時講電話。）

答 2 ： I talk to my friends for a couple of hours each day.
（每天我會和朋友們講個幾小時。）

名師解析

■ on the phone ＝ by phone
■ { a couple ：是表示「一對夫妻」或「一對戀人」
  { a couple of... ：是表示「幾個……」或「二至三個……」。

題20 ： How many meals do you usually have every day?
（你每天通常吃幾餐？）

答 1 ： I eat three meals a day.
（我一天吃三餐。）

答 2： **Every day I eat three meals and have a snack before I go to bed.**

（每天我吃三餐且在上床前會吃消夜。）

亦可回答：　I have 3 regular meals a day, and have snacks between each meal.

（我每天都吃三個正餐，並且在每個正餐間吃點心。）

句型四　Who 為首

題 1： Who is your favorite movie star? Please name one of the movies in which she or he starred.

（你最喜愛的電影明星是誰？請說出一部她或他演的電影名稱。）

答 1： My favorite movie star is Jet Li who starred in "Hero".

（我最喜愛的電影明星是李連杰，他主演《英雄》。）

答 2： Tom Cruise, who acted in "War of the Worlds", is my favorite movie star.

（湯姆克魯斯是我最喜愛的電影明星，他主演《世界大戰》。）

題 2： Who do you look more like, your father or your mother?

（你看起來像誰，像你父親還是你母親？）

答 1： I look more like my father than my mother.

（我看起來比較像爸爸，而比較不像媽媽。）

答 2： I think I look more like my mother than my father.

（我覺得我看起來比較像媽媽，而比較不像爸爸。）

題 3： Who is your favorite teacher? Why do you like him or her?

（誰是你最喜愛的老師？你為什麼喜歡他／她？）

答 1： My favorite teacher is Mr. Lee because he makes history very interesting.

（我最喜愛的老師是李老師，因為他讓歷史變得很有趣。）

答 2： **Miss Wang is my favorite teacher because she makes geometry easy to understand.**

（王老師是我最喜愛的老師，因為她讓幾何學變得容易了解。）

名師解析

■ 在國外，對老師的稱呼會用 Miss、Mr. 及 Mrs.（已婚的女性），再加上姓氏。

題 4： **Who is your best friend? Why?**

（誰是你最好的朋友？為什麼？）

答 1： **Jeff is my best friend because he is always around when I need advice or comfort.**

（傑夫是我最好的朋友，因為在我需要建議或安慰時，他總是在我身邊。）

答 2： **My best friend is Sue. She doesn't tell anyone my secrets.**

（我最好的朋友是蘇。她不會把我的秘密告訴任何人。）

題 5： **Who is the actor you like best? Why?**

（誰是你最喜歡的演員？為什麼？）

答 1： **Stephen Chow is my favorite actor because he is so funny.**

（周星馳是我最喜愛的演員，因為他很滑稽。）

答 2：**There is no specific actor I like best because I don't watch TV or movies a lot.**

（我沒有特定喜歡的演員，因為我不常看電視或電影。）

題 6：**Who is your favorite writer? Name one of his or her books.**

（誰是你最喜歡的作家？說出一本他或她的著作。）

答 1：**I like Shakespeare most. I like his drama -- "Romeo and Juliet".**

（我最喜歡莎士比亞，我喜歡他的戲劇──《羅密歐與茱麗葉》。）

答 2：**My favorite writer is Shakespeare. "A Midsummer Night's Dream" is one of his works.**

（我最喜歡的作家是莎士比亞，《仲夏夜之夢》是他其中一部作品。）

題 7：**Who do you think loves you most ?**

（你認為誰是最愛你的？）

答 1：**Of course, my mom loves me most. Every mother loves her child most.**

（當然是我媽媽最愛我，每個母親都最愛她的小孩。）

答 2：**My parents love me most. Nothing can take the place of my parents' love.**

（我的父母最愛我，沒有任何事物可以取代我父母的愛。）

句型五　When 為首

題 1 ： **When is your birthday?**

（你的生日是什麼時候？）

答 1 ： **June 3, 1978 is my birthday.**

（我的生日是 1978 年 6 月 3 日。）

答 2 ： **My birthday is January 11, 1988.**

（我的生日是 1988 年 1 月 11 日。）

名師解析

■ When is your birthday? = When were you born?

題 2 ： **When was the last time you went to see a movie?**

（你上次看電影是什麼時候？）

答 1 ： **The last time I went to see a movie was last weekend.**

（我上次去看電影是上個週末。）

答 2 ： **I went to see a movie two weeks ago.**

（我二個禮拜前去看電影。）

題 3 ： **When did you leave home this morning? How long did it take to get here?**

（今天早上你何時離開家裡？你花了多久時間來到這裡？）

答 1 ： **I left home at 7 a.m. this morning. It took me half an hour to get here.**

（今天早上我七點離開家，我花了半個小時來這裡。）

答 2 ： **This morning, I left home at 6:30. It only took me 10 minutes to get here.**

（今天早上，我六點三十分離開家，我只花十分鐘就到這裡。）

題 4 ： **When did you begin studying English?**

（你從何時開始學英文？）

答 1 ： **I began studying English in junior high school.**

（我從國中開始學英文。）

答 2 ： **I didn't start studying English until I was in high school.**

（直到我念中學，我才開始學英文。）

名師解析

■ begin = start 開始

■ junior high school ＝ junior high 國中

■ ...not...until... ，直到……，才……

(until = till)。

題 5 ： **When do you go to school or go to work?**

（你幾點去學校或上班？）

答 1 ： **I go to my office around 8:30 a.m.**

（我早上八點三十分去辦公室。）

答 2 ： **My school begins at 7:30 a.m., so I need to go to school before 7:30 a.m.**

（學校是從早上七點半開始，所以我必須在七點半之前到學校。）

名 師 解 析

■ begins at = starts at（從……開始）或反義 ends at...（在……結束）

題 6 ： **When is Christmas?**

（聖誕節在何時？）

答 1 ： **Christmas is on December 25th.**

（聖誕節是在 12 月 25 日。）

答 2 ： **People celebrate the birth of Jesus; it is on December 25th of every year.**

（聖誕節是為了慶祝耶穌的誕生，是在每年的 12 月 25 日那天。）

題 7 ： **When is Chinese New Year?**

（中國新年是在什麼時候？）

答 1 ： **Chinese New Year is the beginning of a lunar calendar.**

（中國新年是農曆年的開始。）

答 2 ： **Chinese New Year is on a different day each year.**

（每年的中國新年是在不同的時間。）

題 8 ： **When do you study on your own?**

（你在什麼時候自己讀書？）

答 1 ： **I can't begin studying until I get home from the cram school at 9 p.m.**

（直到晚上九點我從補習班回到家後，我才能開始自己讀書。）

答 2 ： **I begin studying as soon as I get home.**

（我一回到家就開始讀書。）

題 9 ： **When is the best time to call you?**

（什麼時候是打電話給你的最好時間？）

答 1 ： **The best time to call me is every night after 6 p.m.**

（每晚六點後是打電話給我的最好時間。）

答 2 ： **I do not have a regular schedule; call any time. If no one answers, keep trying.**

（我沒有固定的時間表，任何時候都可以打給我，如果沒有人接就繼續打。）

題 10 ： **When do you usually leave the house for work every morning?**

（你每天早上通常是什麼時候出門去上班？）

答 1 ： **I usually leave the house at 6 a.m. because the bus leaves at 6:30 a.m.**

（我通常六點出門，因為巴士會在六點半時開走。）

答 2 ： **I leave every morning at 7 a.m.**

（我每天早上七點時出門。）

題 11 ： **When was the last time you went out for a date?**

（你上次出去約會是什麼時候？）

答 1 ： **The last time I went out for a date was a year ago.**

（我上次出去約會是在一年前。）

答 2 ： **I don't go out for a date anymore because I already have a girl friend.**

（我不再出去約會了，因為我已經有了女朋友。）

句型六 Where 為首

題 1 ： **Where do you want to go on vacation?**
（你想去哪裡渡假？）

答 1 ： **I want to go on vacation to Thailand.**
（我想去泰國渡假。）

答 2 ： **I really want to go on vacation to America.**
（我真的很想去美國渡假。）

題 2 ： **Where can you see a lot of animals?**
（你可以在那裡看到許多動物？）

答 1 ： **I can see a lot of animals at the zoo.**
（我可以在動物園看到許多動物。）

答 2 ： **My grandpa's farm has a lot of animals.**
（我爺爺的牧場有許多動物。）

名師解析

■ farm (n.) 牧場、農場、農莊

題 3 ： **Where do you usually go when you eat out?**
（當你到外面用餐時，你通常都到哪裡吃？）

答 1 ： **When I eat out, I usually go to McDonald's.**
（當我去外面用餐時，我通常是去麥當勞。）

答 2 ： **We usually go to a cafeteria when we eat out.**
（當我們出去吃飯時，我們通常去自助餐店。）

名師解析

■ cafeteria (n.) 自助餐店

題 4： **Where did you go last weekend?**
（上個週末你去哪裡？）

答 1： **Last weekend I stayed at home.**
（上個週末我待在家裡。）

答 2： **I went to my grandparents' last weekend.**
（上個週末我去我祖父母家。）

**名師解析**

■ grandparents' = grandparents' house

題 5： **Where do you study English?**
（你在哪裡學英文？）

答 1： **I study English only at my school.**
（我只在我的學校學英文。）

答 2： **I go to a cram school to study English.**
（我到補習班學英文。）

題 6： **Where do you like to hang out?**
（你喜歡到哪裡逛？）

答 1： **I like to shop at Tiger City with my family.**
（我喜歡和朋友去老虎城購物。）

答 2 ： **Downtown Taichung is where I like to hang out with my friends.**
（我喜歡和朋友去台中鬧區逛。）

名師解析

■ downtown (n.) 鬧區、市中心

題 7 ： **Where is Hsinchu ?**
（新竹在哪裡？）

答 1 ： **Hsinchu is a city in Taiwan.**
（新竹是台灣的一個城市。）

答 2 ： **Hsinchu is south of Taipei.**
（新竹在台北的南邊。）

題 8 ： **Where is the swimming pool? And how do I get there?**
（請問游泳池在哪裡？我要如何到那裡去？）

答 1 ： **The swimming pool is on Sunset Road. It is 3 blocks east from here.**
（游泳池在日落路上。從這往東走三條街就到了。）

答 2 ： **Sorry, there is no swimming pool near here.**
（對不起，這附近沒有游泳池。）

題 9 ： **Where do you usually go after school?**
（放學後你通常會去哪裡？）

答 1 ： **I usually go home after school and start doing my**

homework.

（我通常放學後就回家，並開始做我的功課。）

答 2： **I usually go to the cyber cafe after school to play online games, and then go back home.**

（放學後我通常會去網咖玩線上遊戲，之後再回家。）

題 10： **Where is the nearest hospital?**

（最近的醫院在哪裡？）

答 1： **The nearest hospital is Taiwan University Medical Hospital. Go north 7 blocks, turn right and you should see it on your left hand side.**

（最近的醫院是台大醫院，往北走七條街後右轉，你就會看到它在你的左手邊。）

答 2： **There is no hospital nearby, but there is a clinic right across the street.**

（附近沒有大醫院，但是對面有一家小診所。）

題 11： **Where do you save your personal savings?**

（你把你的積蓄都存在哪裡？）

答 1： **I save my personal savings in the post office because I can withdraw the money easily.**

（我把我的積蓄都存在郵局裡，因為領錢很方便。）

答 2： **Don't tell anyone I put all my money under my pillow.**

（別告訴任何人，我把我全部的錢存放在我的枕頭下。）

句型七　Which 為首

題 1： **Which language do you speak best, English, Chinese, or Taiwanese?**

（你最會說哪種語言？英文、中文或台語？）

答 1： **I speak Taiwanese best.**

（我台語說得最好。）

答 2： **Chinese is the language I speak best.**

（我說得最好的語言是中文。）

題 2： **Which city or which county are you living in now?**

（你現在住在哪個縣市？）

答 1： **I am living in Taichung City now.**

（我現正住在台中市。）

答 2： **Taipei County is where I live now.**

（我現在住在台北縣。）

名師解析

■ county 在美國是表示「郡」、「行政區」；在台灣是表示「縣」。

題 3： **Which do you like better, city life or country life?**

（你比較喜歡都市生活還是鄉村生活？）

答 1： **I like city life better than country life.**

（我喜歡都市生活多於鄉村生活。）

答 2： I like country life because the air is fresh and there's no traffic jams.

（我喜歡鄉村生活，因為空氣新鮮，而且沒有塞車。）

題 4： Which holiday is your favorite and why?

（你最喜歡那個節日？為什麼？）

答 1： Chinese New Year is my favorite holiday because I like getting red envelopes.

（中國新年是我最喜歡的節日，因為我喜歡拿紅包。）

答 2： My favorite holiday is Christmas because I like getting gifts.

（我最喜歡的節日是聖誕節，因為我喜歡得到禮物。）

題 5： Which do you like better? English or math?

（英文或數學，那一個你比較喜歡？）

答 1： I like English better. I always get good grades in English.

（我比較喜歡英文，我總是可以在英文得到好成績。）

答 2： I prefer math. I am good with numbers.

（我比較喜歡數學，我對數字很拿手。）

題 6： Which country would you like to visit? Why?

（你想去參觀那個國家？為什麼？）

答 1： I would like to visit Europe because I have never been to Europe.

（我想去參觀歐洲，因為我從未去過歐洲。）

答 2 ： **I would like to go to Egypt and see the pyramids.**
（我會想去埃及那看看金字塔。）

題 7 ： **Which do you like better, home-made food or fast food?**
（家庭料理和速食，那一種你比較喜歡？）

答 1 ： **I like home-made food more than fast food. My mom is a good cook.**
（我喜歡家庭料理多於速食。我媽媽很會做菜的。）

答 2 ： **I like fast food more than home-made food.**
（我喜歡速食多於家庭料理。）

題 8 ： **Which soft drink do you like best? Why?**
（你最喜歡哪種飲料？為什麼？）

答 1 ： **I like coca-cola best because it keeps me awake.**
（我最喜歡可口可樂，因為它可以幫助我清醒。）

答 2 ： **I don't like any soft drinks because they are not healthy.**
（我不喜歡任何飲料，因為它們都不健康。）

題 9 ： **Which sport do you like and do the most? Why?**
（你最喜歡並且最常做的是哪種運動？為什麼？）

答 1 ： **I like to play basketball the most because it makes me taller.**
（我喜歡打籃球，因為它可以使我長高。）

答 2：I like all kinds of sports, but I like fencing the most because it requires the most concentration.

（我喜歡各種運動，但是我最喜歡的是西洋劍，因為它最需要集中精神。）

句型八 If 為首／假設的句型

題 1： **If it rains suddenly but you don't have an umbrella, what will you do?**

（假如突然下雨，但你又沒有雨傘，你會怎麼做？）

答 1： **If it rains suddenly but I don't have an umbrella, I will stay inside until it stops raining.**

（要是突然下雨，但我沒有雨傘的話，那在雨停之前我會留在室內。）

答 2： **I will call my mom to pick me up if it rains suddenly and I don't have an umbrella.**

（假如突然下雨而且我沒有雨傘的話，我會打電話請我媽媽來接我。）

題 2： **If you lost your house key, what would you do?**

（假如你房子的鑰匙不見了，你會怎麼做？）

答 1： **If I lost my house key, I would use the key my mom had hidden to get into the house.**

（假如我弄丟我房子的鑰匙，我會用我媽媽藏起來的鑰匙進屋。）

答 2： **I would call my mom if I lost the house key.**

（假如我弄丟了房子的鑰匙，我會打電話給我媽媽。）

名 師 解 析

■ 答1裡，用過去完成式 had hidden 表示在丟掉之前藏的。

題 3： If your friend cheated you, what would you do?

（要是你的朋友欺騙你，你會怎麼做？）

答 1： If my friend cheated me, I would know he wasn't a real friend.

（要是我朋友欺騙我，我就會了解到他並不是真正的朋友。）

答 2： I would get very angry if my friend cheated me.

（要是我的朋友欺騙我的話，我會很生氣。）

題 4： If your friend was going to Japan to study, what would you say to your friend?

（假如你的朋友要去日本留學，你會對你朋友說什麼？）

答 1： Take care! I will miss you. Write me as soon as you get to Japan.

（保重！我會想你的，一到日本就寫信給我。）

答 2： E-mail me. Keep in touch. I will miss you.

（寄電子郵件給我，保持聯絡，我會想你的。）

題 5： If you won a ten-million-dollar lottery, what would you do?

（假如你贏了一千萬元樂透，你會做些什麼？）

答 1： I would take my family on a trip to New Zealand if I won a ten-million-dollar lottery.

（假如我贏了一千萬元樂透，我會帶我家人到紐西蘭旅遊。）

答 2： If I won a ten-million-dollar lottery, I would buy my own boat, and invite all of my friends for a ride.

（假如我贏了一千萬元樂透，我會用來買我自己的船，並邀請所有朋友去兜風。）

題 6 ： **If you saw a little girl crying on the street, what would you ask her?**

（假如你看到一個小女孩在路上哭泣，你會問她什麼？）

答 1 ： **If I saw a little girl on the street crying, I would ask her if she was lost.**

（假如我看到一個小女孩在路上哭泣，我就會問她是不是迷路了。）

答 2 ： **If I saw a little girl crying on the street, I would ask her why she was crying.**

（假如我看見一個小女孩在路上哭泣，我會問她為什麼哭。）

題 7 ： **If you lost your way to the train station, how would you ask someone for directions?**

（假如你在往火車站的路上迷路了，你會如何向人問路？）

答 1 ： **If I lost my way to the train station, I would ask someone, "How can I get to the train station from here?"**

（假如我在往火車站的路上迷路了，我會問人說：「請問我要如何從這裡到火車站？」）

答 2 ： **If I got lost on my way to the train station, I would ask someone, "Where is the train station?"**

（假如我在往火車站的路上迷路了，我會問人說：「請問火車站在哪裡？」）

題 8 ： **If someone asks you how to get to the museum, how would you answer him?**

（假如有人問你去博物館的路要如何去，你會如何回答他？）

答 1 ： **If someone asks me how to go to the museum, I would say, "I'm sorry. I don't know how to get to the museum."**

（假如有人問我去博物館的路，我會說：「很抱歉，我不知道要如何去博物館。」）

答 2 ： **If someone asks me how to get to the museum, I would tell him the museum is across the street from the city police station.**

（假如有人問我要如何去博物館，我會告訴他博物館在市警局對面。）

題 9 ： **If you won two free tickets to travel abroad, who would you invite to go with you?**

（假如你贏得二張免費國外旅遊機票，你會邀誰和你一起去？）

答 1 ： **I would invite either of my parents to go with me.**

（我會邀請我父母其中一人和我一起去。）

答 2 ： **I would invite one of my best friends to travel with me.**

（我會邀我最好的朋友們中的一個和我一起旅行。）

題 10 ： **If you could live anywhere in the world, where would you live?**

（如果你能住在世界上的任何一個地方，你想住在哪裡？）

答 1 ： If I could live anywhere in the world, I would live in Japan.
（如果我能住在世界上的任何一個地方，我想住在日本。）

答 2 ： I would live in Switzerland if I could live anywhere in the world.
（如果我能住在世界上的任何一個地方，我想住在瑞士。）

題11 ： If you found a suitcase with ten million dollars inside, what would you do?
（假如你發現一個手提箱裡面有一千萬元，你會怎麼做？）

答 1 ： If I found a suitcase with ten million dollars inside, I would start an orphanage.
（假如我發現一個手提箱裡面有一千萬元，我會創辦一個孤兒院。）

答 2 ： I would support my parents so they didn't have to work if I found a suitcase with ten million dollars inside.
（假如我發現一個手提箱裡面有一千萬元，我會用來養我父母，那麼他們就可以不用工作了。）

題12 ： If you had one wish to make, what would it be?
（假如你可以許一個願望，那會是什麼？）

答 1 ： If I had one wish to make, I would wish I were the most beautiful girl in the world .
（假如我可以許一個願望，我希望變成世界上最美的女孩。）

答 2 ： I would wish that there were no sickness in this world, if I had one wish to make.

（假如我可以許一個願望，我希望這個世界沒有疾病。）

名 師 解 析

■ 答 1 與答 2 裡的 were 是用過去式表示與現在事實相反的假設。

句型九　Why 為首

題 1 ： **Why are you here?**

（你為什麼在這裡？）

答 1 ： **I came here because I am taking a GEPT test.**

（我會在這裡是因為我正在參加全民英檢考試。）

答 2 ： **I am here because I have to take a GEPT test.**

（我在這裡是因為我必須參加英檢考試。）

題 2 ： **Why don't people have to work or go to school on October 10ᵗʰ?**

（在 10 月 10 日，為什麼人們不用去上班或上課？）

答 1 ： **People don't go to work or school on October 10ᵗʰ in Taiwan because it is Taiwan's national holiday.**

（在台灣，10 月 10 日人們不用上班或上課，因為那天是台灣的國定假日。）

答 2 ： **Because October 10ᵗʰ is our national holiday, people don't go to work or school on that day.**

（因為 10 月 10 日是我們的國定假日，在那天人們不用上班或上課。）

題 3 ： **Why do you want to study English?**

（你為什麼想學英文？）

答 1 ： **I want to study English so that I can get a good job.**

（我想學英文是為了可以找到好工作。）

答 2 ： **I want to move to America when I am an adult, so I want to study English.**

（在我長大成人後，我想搬去美國，所以我想學英文。）

名 師 解 析

■ adult (n.) 成年人、成年的。「A片」中的 A 即是 adult 的字首，adult movie 表示「成人電影」。

題 4 ： **Why do you want to take the GEPT test?**

（你為什麼想參加全民英檢測驗？）

答 1 ： **I want to take the GEPT test. If I pass it, I can get a raise at my job.**

（我想參加全民英檢測驗，是因為要是我通過考試，我就可獲加薪。）

答 2 ： **I want to take the GEPT test to see if my English is good enough.**

（我想參加全民英檢測驗，是想要知道我的英文是否夠好。）

名 師 解 析

■ 本題題目的意思同下二者：

　　(1) What is the reason you want to take the GEPT test?

　　(2) What do you want to take the GEPT test for?

■ raise (n.) 提高、加薪

題 5 ： **Why do you walk instead of driving to work?**

（你為什麼不開車反而走路上班呢？）

答 1 ： **I walk to work instead of driving because I want to exercise so that I don't get fat.**

（我不開車反而走路上班是因為我想做點運動，這樣我才不會變胖。）

答 2 ： **The gas price is too high and the bus is too crowed, so I walk to work.**

（汽油的價錢太高而公車又太擠了，所以我走路上班。）

題 6 ： **Why do you drink tea but not coffee?**

（為什麼你喝茶而不喝咖啡呢？）

答 1 ： **I drink tea but not coffee because coffee is bitter.**

（我喝茶而不喝咖啡是因為咖啡比較苦。）

答 2 ： **Tea has less caffeine than coffee. If I drink coffee, I can't sleep.**

（茶的咖啡因比咖啡少，如果我喝咖啡的話我會睡不著。）

題 7 ： **Why did you make that little girl cry?**

（你為什麼把那個小女孩弄哭了？）

答 1 ： **I don't know why she cried, I just waved at her.**

（我不知道她為什麼哭了，我只有對她招招手而已。）

答 2 ： **She was pulling my hair and I told her to stop, maybe I spoke to her too loudly.**

（可能我對她說話太大聲了，因為她一直拉著我的頭髮，而我叫她不要這樣。）

題 8 ： Why didn't you learn English well in high school?
（為什麼你在中學時沒有把英文學好？）

答 1 ： I didn't learn English well in high school because my English teacher never cared about me.
（我在中學時沒有把英文學好是因為我的英文老師從來沒有在乎過我。）

答 2 ： I skipped a lot of classes, and that's why I didn't learn my English well.
（因為我翹了很多課，所以沒有把我的英文學好。）

句型十　以原形動詞為為首的祈使句
有時前／後加了「please」

　　基本上原型動詞為首的話，就是發問者要求聽話者做某事，即是所謂的祈使句。句子的前後是否加 please 皆可，那只是禮貌的表達而已，不影響整個句的本意。

題 1 ： **Please talk about yourself.**
（請談談你自己。）

答 1 ： **I am a student in my second year of senior high school. My favorite subject is math, and I hope to be a math teacher in the future. I like to play basketball.**
（我是一個高中二年級的學生。我最愛的科目是數學，我希望將來成為一個數學老師。我喜歡打籃球。）

答 2 ： **I am a junior high student. I like to study English and watch English movies. I also like to read.**
（我是一個國中生，我喜歡學英文和看英文電影，同時我也喜歡閱讀。）

名 師 解 析

■ 本題題目的意思同： Introduce yourself shortly.

題 2 ： **Please say something about the weather today.**
（請說一些有關於今天天氣的事。）

答 1 ： **The weather is cold today, but the sky is clear and the sun is shining.**

（今天的天氣很冷，但是天空很晴朗且太陽很耀眼。）

答 2 ： **It is raining very hard today. I hope to go back home soon.**

（今天雨下得很大。我希望快點回家。）

題 3 ： **Please count from eleven to twenty.**

（請從 11 數到 20 。）

答 1 ： **Eleven, twelve, thirteen, fourteen, fifteen, sixteen, seventeen, eighteen, nineteen, twenty.**

（11、12、13、14、15、16、17、18、19、20。）

名師解析

■ 在學習指南裡，命題中心很明顯地告知考生，一定要能清楚說出數字，而很多考生13及30、14及40等無法清楚區分，所以本題是極有可能出現。

題 4 ： **Please name as many English girls' names that are flowers.**

（請儘可能的說出是英文女子名同時也是花的名字的字。）

答 1 ： **The English girls' names that are flowers are Jasmine, Daisy, Rose and Lily.**

（女生英文名是花名的有茉莉、雛菊、薔薇和百合。）

答 2 ： **Like Violet, Rose, Lily, Jasmine and so on.**

（像紫蘿蘭、玫瑰、百合、茉莉等等。）

題 5 ： Describe your neighborhood, please.

（請描述你的鄰近街坊。）

答 1 ： I live in an apartment. On the first floor of our apartment building, there is a bank. Besides, there are many convenience stores nearby.

（我住在一間公寓，我們公寓大樓的一樓有一家銀行，除此之外，在我們附近也有許多家便利商店。）

答 2 ： Our neighbors are all very kind and friendly. We live in a small village. Most of us know each other. Though it is not a big city, it is convenient to live here.

（我們的街坊鄰居都非常和善親切，我們住在一個小村莊，許多人都彼此認識，雖然不是個大城市，但住在這裏還滿方便的。）

題 6 ： Please talk about anything you are good at.

（請談談任何你所擅長的。）

答 1 ： I am good at music. I can play many musical instruments such as piano, guitar, drum and so on.

（我擅長音樂，我會許多樂器，像鋼琴、吉他、鼓等等。）

答 2 ： What I am good at is machines. It is easy for me to take something apart and put it back together again.

（我擅長的是與機械有關的事物，我可以很輕易的把東西拆開，再組回去。）

名 師 解 析

such as... = like... 像是……
for example 舉例而言
for instance 舉例而言
■ and so on = and so forth 等等之類的

題 7 ： Tell me an unforgettable experiences of yours, please?
（告訴我一件你難忘的經歷。）

答 1 ： **An unforgettable experience happened to me when I was just 6. I got lost in a large department store.**
（我難忘的經歷發生在我只有六歲的時候，我在一家大百貨公司迷路。）

答 2 ： **I will never forget my first visit to the dentist when I was 8 years old.**
（我永遠不會忘記八歲時第一次去看牙醫。）

題 8 ： Please tell me the most embarrassing thing that you have done in your life.
（請告訴我你這一生中做過最丟臉的事情。）

答 1 ： **The most embarrassing thing that I have done in my life was to recognize the wrong person on the street.**
（我這一生中做過最丟臉的一件事是我在路上認錯人。）

答 2 ： **I got caught cheating in an exam and was told to stop taking the test. That was the most embarrassing moment in my life.**

（我在一個考試中被抓到作弊而且被要求停止考試，那是我這一生中最丟臉的事。）

口說模擬試題及解答

口說模擬試題第一回【試題】

請在十五秒內完成並唸出下列自我介紹的句子：

My test number is <u>（初試准考證號碼）</u> , and my seat number is <u>（口試座位號碼）</u> .

第一部份：複誦

　　共五題。題目不印在試卷上，經由耳機播出，每題播出兩次，兩次之間大約有一至二秒的間隔。聽完兩次後，請立即複誦一次。

第二部分：朗讀句子與短文

　　共有五個句子及一篇短文，請先利用一分鐘的時間閱讀試卷上的句子與短文，然後在一分鐘內以正常的速度，清楚正確的朗讀一遍。

> One: I've got to go now.
>
> Two: Could you do me a favor, please?
>
> Three: What's wrong with your car?
>
> Four: May I be excused? I will be back soon.
>
> Five: Please leave your message, and I will call you later.
>
> Six: Teddy was late for school again. Worst of all, Teddy forgot to bring his homework. His teacher was really mad. The teacher called his mom and complained about him. His mom said that she was

too busy to wake hIm up or help him with his homework. She felt sorry for what happened.

第三部份：回答問題

　　共七題。題目不印在試卷上，經由耳機播出，每題播出兩次，兩次之間約有一至二秒的間隔。聽完兩次後，請立即回答，每題回答時間為十五秒，請在作答時間內儘量的表達。

※請將下列自我介紹的句子再唸一遍，請開始：

My test number is ＿（初試准考證號碼）＿, and my seat number is ＿（口試座位號碼）＿.

口說模擬試題第一回【解答】

請在十五秒內完成並唸出下列自我介紹的句子：

My test number is ___339162___ , and my seat number is ___475803___.
（虛擬初試准考證號碼）　　　　　　　　　　　　　　　　　　（虛擬口試座位號碼）

第一部份：複誦

　　共五題。題目不印在試卷上，經由耳機播出，每題播出兩次，兩次之間大約有一至二秒的間隔。聽完兩次後，請立即複誦一次。

1. There are 50 states in America.

（美國有五十個州。）

2. I didn't sleep until 12 o'clock.

（直到十二點，我才睡覺。）

3. My grandmother enjoys taking walks every evening.

（我奶奶喜歡在每天傍晚時散步。）

4. Take it easy; we still have a lot of time left.

（放輕鬆，我們還剩很多時間。）

5. Please feel free to call me if you have any questions.

（假如你有任何問題，請勿拘束隨時可打電話給我。）

第二部分：朗讀句子與短文

　　共有五個句子及一篇短文，請先利用一分鐘的時間閱讀試卷上的句子與短文，然後在一分鐘內以正常的速度，清楚正確的朗讀一遍。

One: ❸❷ ❸ ❶ ❹ ❸
I've got to go now.

（我現在必須走了。）

Two: ❷ ❸ ❷ ❸❶❷❸ ❹
Could you do me a favor, please?

（可請你幫我一個忙嗎？）

Three: ❷ ❸ ❷ ❸ ❹
What's wrong with your car?

（你的車子怎麼了？）

Four: ❷❸❷ ❹ ❸❷ ❶ ❹ ❸
May I be excused? I will be back soon.

（請容許我先離開，我會儘快回來的。）

Five: ❷ ❹ ❸ ❹ ❶❷❷ ❹ ❷ ❹
Please leave your message, and I will call you later.

（請留言，稍後我將回電。）

Six: ❹ ❸ ❸ ❷ ❹ ❸ ❹ ❷ ❹ ❹
Teddy was late for school again. Worst of all, Teddy
❹ ❷ ❸ ❸ ❸ ❷ ❸ ❸
forgot to bring his homework. His teacher was
❹ ❹ ❶ ❷ ❸ ❷ ❹ ❷
really mad. The teacher called his mom and
❹ ❶ ❷ ❷ ❹ ❹ ❷
complained about him. His mom said that she was
❹ ❹ ❷ ❹ ❸ ❸ ❷ ❹ ❸ ❸ ❶
too busy to wake him up or help him with his
❸ ❹ ❷ ❷ ❸ ❶ ❹ ❹
homework. She felt sorry for what happened.

（泰迪上學又遲到了，最糟糕的是，泰迪忘了帶他的家庭
作業。他的老師很生氣，打電話跟他母親並抱怨關於泰
迪的狀況。他母親說她太忙了，以致於不能叫他起床或
幫他注意家庭作業。她為發生的事感到很抱歉。）

第三部份：回答問題

　　共七題。題目不印在試卷上，經由耳機播出，每題播出兩次，兩次之間約有一至二秒的間隔。聽完兩次後，請立即回答，每題回答時間為十五秒，請在作答時間內儘量的表達。

　　※以下"Q"為耳機播出的題目，"A"與"B"為作者提供讀者的回答範例。

1.Q：Do you like to live in the city or in the country? Why?
（你喜歡住在城市還是鄉下？為什麼？）

A：I like to live in the country because it is so quiet and peaceful.
（我喜歡住在鄉下，因為鄉下十分寧靜且祥和。）

B：I like to live in the city because everything is so convenient.
（我喜歡住在城市，因為每件事物都很方便。）

2.Q：What kind of person would you like to marry?
（你想和什麼樣的人結婚？）

A：I would like to marry a rich man.
（我想嫁給有錢人。）

B：I would like to marry a doctor.
（我想跟醫生結婚。）

3.Q：Who did you see first today after you woke up?

（你今天起床後第一個看到的人是誰？）

A： My mom woke me up this morning so she was the first person I saw.

（今天早上是我母親叫我起床，所以她是我第一個看到的人。）

B： I saw my dad first this morning when I walked out of my bedroom.

（今天早上當我走出臥房時，我第一眼看到的是我爸爸。）

4.Q： When were you born?

（你什麼時候出生？）

A： I was born on November 7th, 1985.

（我是 1985 年 11 月 7 日出生。）

B： I was born at 6:05 p.m. on October 14th, 1990.

（我是 1990 年 10 月 14 日晚上六點五分出生。）

5.Q： Where do you usually eat breakfast?

（你通常在哪裡吃早餐？）

A： I usually eat breakfast at the breakfast shop.

（我通常在早餐店吃早餐。）

B： My mom usually fixes me breakfast so I eat at home.

（我母親通常都會準備早餐，所以我在家裡吃。）

6.Q： What time do you usually get out of class or the office?

（你通常幾點離開教室或辦公室？）

A：I am a high school student. I usually get out of class at 4:30 p.m.

（我是高中生，我通常在下午四點半下課離開。）

B：I usually get out of my office at 5 o'clock p.m. But sometimes I have to work overtime until around 6 o'clock p.m.

（我通常在下午五點離開辦公室，但有時候我需要加班到晚上六點左右。）

7.Q：How many people are there in your family?

（你家有幾個人？）

A：There are seven people in my family. Besides my parents, there are my four siblings.

（我家有七個人，除了我父母外，有四個兄弟姐妹。）

B：There are six people in my family. They are my grandparents, my parents, my younger brother, and me.

（我家有六個人，有我的祖父母、父母、弟弟和我。）

口說模擬試題第二回【試題】

請在十五秒內完成並唸出下列自我介紹的句子：

My test number is （初試准考證號碼）, and my seat number is （口試座位號碼）.

第一部份：複誦

共五題。題目不印在試卷上，經由耳機播出，每題播出兩次，兩次之間大約有一至二秒的間隔。聽完兩次後，請立即複誦一次。

第二部分：朗讀句子與短文

共有五個句子及一篇短文，請先利用一分鐘的時間閱讀試卷上的句子與短文，然後在一分鐘內以正常的速度，清楚正確的朗讀一遍。

   One: Have you ever been abroad?

   Two: May I take your order right now?

 Three: The roast beef was really delicious.

  Four: He arrived at the gym 20 minutes later than she did.

  Five: I was born on April 5th, 1991.

   Six: English is an international language. The official language of many countries is English. People all over the world speak English as their second language. They often speak English when they are

doing business, or when they are traveling.

Perhaps, your English is not good. However, if you practice every day, you will improve little by little.

第三部份：回答問題

　　共七題。題目不印在試卷上，經由耳機播出，每題播出兩次，兩次之間約有一至二秒的間隔。聽完兩次後，請立即回答，每題回答時間為十五秒，請在作答時間內儘量的表達。

※請將下列自我介紹的句子再唸一遍，請開始：

My test number is ＿（初試准考證號碼）＿ , and my seat number is ＿（口試座位號碼）＿ .

口說模擬試題第二回【解答】

請在十五秒內完成並唸出下列自我介紹的句子：

My test number is ___943028___ , and my seat number is ___661755___ .

（虛擬初試准考證號碼）　　　　　　　　　　　　　　（虛擬口試座位號碼）

第一部份：複誦

共五題。題目不印在試卷上，經由耳機播出，每題播出兩次，兩次之間大約有一至二秒的間隔。聽完兩次後，請立即複誦一次。

1. Go ahead, please

（請繼續下去。）

2. You are so sweet!

（你好甜美可愛／親切善良！）

3. Where are you going now?

（你現在要去哪？）

4. I have heard a lot about you.

（我聽過很多有關你的事／久仰久仰。）

5. I would like to order a steak with mashed potatoes.

（我想點一客附馬鈴薯泥的牛排。）

第二部分：朗讀句子與短文

共有五個句子及一篇短文，請先利用一分鐘的時間閱讀試卷上的句子與短文，然後在一分鐘內以正常的速度，清楚正確的朗讀一遍。

One: Have you ever been abroad?

（你曾出國過嗎？）

Two: May I take your order right now?

（我現在可以幫你點餐嗎？）

Three: The roast beef was really delicious.

（烤牛肉真的很美味。）

Four: He arrived at the gym 20 minutes later than she did.

（他比她晚 20 分鐘到健身房。）

Five: I was born on April 5th, 1991.

（我是在 1991 年 4 月 5 日出生。）

Six: English is an international language. The official language of many countries is English. People all over the world speak English as their second language. They often speak English when they are doing business, or when they are traveling. Perhaps, your English is not good. However, if you practice every day, you will improve little by little.

（英文是國際語言，許多國家的官方語言都是英文，世界各地的人們都以英文為第二語言。在作生意或是旅行的時候他們通常說英文。或許，你的英文不是很好，然而，如果你每天練習，你將慢慢地進步。）

名師解析

■ throughout = all over 表示 "遍及"。

第三部份：回答問題

　　共七題。題目不印在試卷上，經由耳機播出，每題播出兩次，兩次之間約有一至二秒的間隔。聽完兩次後，請立即回答，每題回答時間為十五秒，請在作答時間內儘量的表達。

　　※以下 "Q" 為耳機播出的題目， "A" 與 "B" 為作者提供讀者的回答範例。

1.Q：**Have you ever been to a zoo? What animals did you see there?**
（你去過動物園嗎？在那你看到了那些動物？）

　A：**Of course I have. I saw tigers, lions and zebras.**
（當然我有去過。我看到了老虎、獅子和斑馬。）

　B：**Yes, I've been to Mucha Zoo many times. I saw a lot of animals, for example, monkeys, gorillas, hippos, elephants and so on.**
（有的，我去過木柵動物園好幾次了。我看到了很多動物，像是猴子、猩猩、河馬和大象等等。）

2.Q：**Where are you going after you take the test?**
（你考完試後會去哪裡？）

A ： I am going to the cram school after I take the test.

（考試後我要去補習班補習。）

B ： My mom will pick me up and I am going home to take a nap.

（我母親會來接我，我將回家休息一下。）

3.Q ： How often do you have your hair washed?

（你多久洗一次頭髮？）

A ： I wash my hair every other day. During the summer time, I wash my hair every day.

（我每隔一天洗一次頭髮；夏天時，我是每天都洗頭髮。）

B ： I always have my hair washed at the hair salon every 3 days in winter, and every other day in summer.

（冬天時，我每三天就到美髮沙龍店洗頭；在夏天我每隔一天就洗一次頭髮。）

4.Q ： Please tell me when Mother's Day is.

（請告訴我母親節是哪一天？）

A ： I only know that Mother's Day is in May.

（我只知道母親節在五月份。）

B ： Mother's Day is the second Sunday in May.

（母親節是在五月的第二個星期天。）

5.Q ： Are you busy tomorrow? What will you do?

（你明天忙嗎？你要做什麼？）

A： No, I am not busy tomorrow because tomorrow is Sunday. I don't have to go anywhere.

（不，明天我不忙，因為明天是星期日，我那裡都不用去。）

B： Yes, I am busy tomorrow. Tomorrow is Sunday and I always go to church on Sunday.

（是，我明天會忙。明天是星期日，星期日我總是去做禮拜。）

名師解析

■ go to church 不等於 go to the church，前者表示「做禮拜」，後者表示「去教會」。就像 go to school 不等於 go to the school，前者為「上學」，後者為「去學校」後者指單純去此建築物而已。

6.Q： What do you look like?

（你外表長的怎樣？）

A： I have black hair, brown eyes, and I wear glasses.

（我有黑色的頭髮、棕色眼睛，而且我有戴眼鏡。）

B： I am young. And I look pretty tall and a little bit thin.

（我很年輕，看起來很高且有點瘦。）

7.Q： What do you do when you catch a cold?

（你感冒時都怎麼處理？）

A： When I catch a cold, I drink a lot of water and sleep a lot.

（當我感冒時，我會多喝水及多睡覺。）

B： **I take lots of vitamin C and drink lots of water when I catch a cold.**

（當我感冒時，我會攝取大量維他命 C 及多喝水。）

口說模擬試題第三回【試題】

請在十五秒內完成並唸出下列自我介紹的句子：

My test number is （初試准考證號碼）, and my seat number is （口試座位號碼）.

第一部份：複誦

共五題。題目不印在試卷上，經由耳機播出，每題播出兩次，兩次之間大約有一至二秒的間隔。聽完兩次後，請立即複誦一次。

第二部分：朗讀句子與短文

共有五個句子及一篇短文，請先利用一分鐘的時間閱讀試卷上的句子與短文，然後在一分鐘內以正常的速度，清楚正確的朗讀一遍。

One: Nice to meet you, Mr. Chen.

Two: I would like to introduce you to my parents.

Three: The shirt cost fifteen hundred dollars and the pants cost five thousand dollars.

Four: He told me he was always very bored when we were together.

Five: The restaurant is on the ninth floor of this building.

Six: Peter has put on a lot of weight lately. He weighs ninety kilograms now. He is afraid his classmates

will laugh at him. He hates going to school. A doctor gave him some good advice, and he decided to go on a diet. He does not eat any junk food any more. He exercises a lot every day. He hopes to lose at least fifteen kilograms.

第三部份：回答問題

共七題。題目不印在試卷上，經由耳機播出，每題播出兩次，兩次之間約有一至二秒的間隔。聽完兩次後，請立即回答，每題回答時間為十五秒，請在作答時間內儘量的表達。

※請將下列自我介紹的句子再唸一遍，請開始：

My test number is <u>（初試准考證號碼）</u> , and my seat number is <u>（口試座位號碼）</u> .

口說模擬試題第三回【解答】

請在十五秒內完成並唸出下列自我介紹的句子：

My test number is ＿＿040651＿＿ , and my seat number is ＿＿832997＿＿.
（虛擬初試准考證號碼）　　　　　　　　　　　　　（虛擬口試座位號碼）

第一部份：複誦

　　共五題。題目不印在試卷上，經由耳機播出，每題播出兩次，兩次之間大約有一至二秒的間隔。聽完兩次後，請立即複誦一次。

1. It's my pleasure.

（這是我的榮幸。）

2. Look! It is snowing.

（看啊！下雪了。）

3. I would like to have fruit salad.

（我想吃水果沙拉。）

4. Hurry up! We are going to be late.

（快點！我們要遲到了。）

5. Have you ever been to America?

（你曾經去過美國嗎？）

第二部分：朗讀句子與短文

　　共有五個句子及一篇短文，請先利用一分鐘的時間閱讀試卷上的句子與短文，然後在一分鐘內以正常的速度，清楚正確的朗讀一遍。

One: Nice to meet you, Mr. Chen.

（陳先生，很高興認識你。）

Two: I would like to introduce you to my parents.

（我想介紹你給我的父母。）

Three: The shirt cost fifteen hundred dollars and the pants cost five thousand dollars.

（這件襯衫花了一千五百元，這褲子花了五千元。）

Four: He told me he was always very bored when we were together.

（當我們在一起的時候，他跟我說他總是很無聊。）

Five: The restaurant is on the ninth floor of this building.

（餐廳是在這棟大樓的9樓。）

Six: Peter has put on a lot of weight lately. He weighs ninety kilograms now. He is afraid his classmates will laugh at him. He hates going to school. A doctor gave him some good advice, and he decided to go on a diet. He does not eat any junk food any more. He exercises a lot every day. He hopes to lose at least fifteen kilograms.

（彼得最近體重增加了，他量體重有九十公斤，他擔心他的同學嘲笑他，他厭惡上學。因醫生給他忠告，他決定節制飲食。他不再吃任何垃圾食物，每天做很多運動，他希望至少減重十五公斤。）

第三部份：回答問題

共七題。題目不印在試卷上，經由耳機播出，每題播出兩次，兩次之間大約有一至二秒的間隔。聽完兩次後，請立即回答，每題回答時間為十五秒，請在作答時間內儘量的表達。

※以下"Q"為耳機播出的題目，"A"與"B"為作者提供讀者的回答範例。

1.Q：What did you have for breakfast this morning?
（今天早餐你吃什麼？）

A：This morning, I only had a sandwich for breakfast.
（今天早上，我只吃一個三明治當早餐。）

B：For breakfast this morning, I had oatmeal with my family.
（今天的早餐，我和家人一起吃燕麥片。）

2.Q：How many times do you brush your teeth every day?
（每天你刷幾次牙？）

A：I brush my teeth every night before I go to bed.
（我在每晚上床睡覺前刷牙。）

B： I brush my teeth three times a day. I brush them after every meal.

（我在三餐飯後都會刷牙。）

3.Q： Where do you like to study? Why?

（你喜歡在什麼地方讀書？為什麼？）

A： I like to study at McDonald's because I like to drink their orange juice while I am studying.

（我喜歡在麥當勞讀書，因我喜歡一邊喝他們的柳橙汁一邊讀書。）

B： I go to the library when I study because it is very quiet there.

（我讀書時喜歡到圖書館去，因為那裡非常安靜。）

4.Q： If you wanted to go to the city library, but you got lost, how would you ask someone for directions?

（假如你要去市立圖書館，但是你迷路了，你要如何跟別人問路？）

A： Excuse me, sir. I am lost. I want to go to the city library. Could you please tell me how to get there?

（先生請問一下，我迷路了，但我想要去市立圖書館，請問你可以告訴我怎麼走嗎？）

B： Excuse me, sir. I would like to go to the city library, but I am lost and don't know how to get there. Can you please show me how to get there?

（先生請問一下，我想去市立圖書館，但是我迷路了，不知道怎麼去，可以請你告訴我該怎麼去嗎？）

5.Q：**What kind of birthday gifts have you received, and which one do you like most?**

（你收過那些生日禮物，你最喜歡哪一個？）

　A：**I have received a CD player, a DVD player, and a bicycle for my birthdays. I like the DVD player most.**

（我收過的生日禮物有CD播放機、DVD播放機及腳踏車，我最喜歡的是DVD播放機。）

　B：**For my birthday, my parents have given me books, clothes, and make-up. I like receiving clothes most.**

（至於我的生日，我父母送過我書本、衣服及化妝品。我最喜歡收到的禮物是衣服。）

6.Q：**If you saw a group of children playing on the street, what would you say to stop them?**

（假如你看到一群小孩在街上玩遊戲，你會說什麼來阻止他們？）

　A：**I would say to the children playing on the street, "It's dangerous to play on the street. Why don't you play at the park instead?"**

（我可以告訴在街上玩遊戲的孩子：「在街道遊戲很危險，為什麼你們不去公園裡玩耍呢？」）

　B：**To the group of children playing on the street, I**

would say, "This street is really busy. You need to play somewhere that is safer."

（對一群在街上玩遊戲的孩子，我會說：「這條街道真的很繁忙，你們應該去一個較安全的地方玩耍。」）

7.Q：**What time is it now?**

（現在幾點了？）

A：**It's a quarter past nine.**

（現在是九點十五分。）

B：**It's 2:30 p.m.**

（現在是下午二點三十分。）

名師解析

■ quarter 表示「四分之一」或「15分鐘」。

■ 除了 It's 幾點鐘 + 幾分 來表達時間之外，時間的表達另有二種：

(1) It's + 分鐘 + to + 點鐘，表示還有幾分鐘就到幾點

(2) It's + 分鐘 + past / after + 點鐘，表示是幾點又過幾分鐘

口說模擬試題第四回【試題】

請在十五秒內完成並唸出下列自我介紹的句子：

My test number is （初試准考證號碼）, and my seat number is （口試座位號碼）.

第一部份：複誦

共五題。題目不印在試卷上，經由耳機播出，每題播出兩次，兩次之間大約有一至二秒的間隔。聽完兩次後，請立即複誦一次。

第二部分：朗讀句子與短文

共有五個句子及一篇短文，請先利用一分鐘的時間閱讀試卷上的句子與短文，然後在一分鐘內以正常的速度，清楚正確的朗讀一遍。

One: Hope to see you soon!

Two: We were all surprised at the news.

Three: How have you been recently?

Four: Don't forget to turn off the air conditioner before you leave.

Five: There are two semesters in a school year in Taiwan.

Six: There is a big sale in the department store. All the items for the past season are 40% off. It means that the price was one thousand dollars, but now it is only six hundred dollars. Mrs. Huang bought a skirt for only sixteen hundred dollars. It used to be twenty seven hundred dollars. She saved nine hundred dollars.

第三部份：回答問題

　　共七題。題目不印在試卷上，經由耳機播出，每題播出兩次，兩次之間約有一至二秒的間隔。聽完兩次後，請立即回答，每題回答時間為十五秒，請在作答時間內儘量的表達。

※請將下列自我介紹的句子再唸一遍，請開始：

My test number is （初試准考證號碼）, and my seat number is （口試座位號碼）.

口說模擬試題第四回【解答】

請在十五秒內完成並唸出下列自我介紹的句子：

My test number is ___295048___ , and my seat number is ___006171___ .
（虛擬初試准考證號碼）　　　　　　　　　　　（虛擬口試座位號碼）

第一部份：複誦

共五題。題目不印在試卷上，經由耳機播出，每題播出兩次，兩次之間大約有一至二秒的間隔。聽完兩次後，請立即複誦一次。

1. Are you sure?

（你確定嗎？）

2. May I talk to Lynn, please?

（我可以跟琳講話嗎？）

3. Come on! You are kidding me!

（少來！你在開我玩笑吧！）

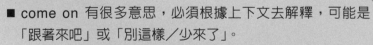

名師解析

■ come on 有很多意思，必須根據上下文去解釋，可能是「跟著來吧」或「別這樣／少來了」。

4. My trip to Taipei was really terrible.

（我去台北的這一趟旅行真的很糟。）

5. Could you tell me how to go to the train station?

（你能告訴我如何去火車站嗎？）

第二部分：朗讀句子與短文

共有五個句子及一篇短文，請先利用一分鐘的時間閱讀試卷上的句子與短文，然後在一分鐘內以正常的速度，清楚正確的朗讀一遍。

One: Hope to see you soon!
（希望能快點見到你！）

Two: We were all surprised at the news.
（我們都對那則新聞感到驚訝。）

Three: How have you been recently?
（你最近好嗎？）

Four: Don't forget to turn off the air conditioner before you leave.
（在你離開前，別忘了關掉冷氣機。）

Five: There are two semesters in a school year in Taiwan.
（在台灣一學年有兩個學期。）

Six: There is a big sale in the department store. All the items for the past season are 40% off. It means that the price was one thousand dollars, but now it is only six hundred dollars. Mrs. Huang bought a skirt for only sixteen hundred dollars. It used to be twenty seven hundred dollars. She saved nine hundred dollars.

（在百貨公司有一場大拍賣，所有上一季的商品都打六
折。意思就是原價一千元，現在只要六百元。黃太太買
了一條裙子只要一千六百元，它原來要二千七百元，她
省了九百元。）

第三部份：回答問題

共七題。題目不印在試卷上，經由耳機播出，每題播出兩次，
兩次之間約有一至二秒的間隔。聽完兩次後，請立即回答，每題回
答時間為十五秒，請在作答時間內儘量的表達。

※以下 "Q" 為耳機播出的題目， "A" 與 "B" 為作者提供
讀者的回答範例。

1.Q： **What are you wearing today?**
（你今天穿什麼？）

A： **Today I'm wearing jeans and a T-shirt.**
（我今天穿牛仔褲和T恤。）

B： **I'm dressed up today and I am wearing a suit.**
（我今天特別打扮，我穿套裝／西裝。）

2.Q： **How much time do you spend on the cell phone a
day?**
（你每天花多少時間講行動電話？）

A： **I don't spend a lot of time on the cell phone. If I do,
my parents will get angry.**

102

（我不會花太多時間在行動電話上，假如我講太久，我父母會生氣。）

B： I usually talk to my girl friend for an hour a day.
（我每天通常都會跟我女朋友講一個小時。）

3.**Q**： Who did you eat dinner with last night?
（你昨晚和誰共進晚餐？）

A： Last night I ate dinner with my friend, Joe.
（昨晚我和我的朋友喬一起吃晚餐。）

B： Nobody！I ate dinner alone last night at my dorm.
（沒有人跟我一起吃，昨晚我獨自一人在我宿舍吃晚餐。）

4.**Q**： Where is your hometown?
（你的故鄉在哪裡？）

A： My hometown is in Hsinchu. I was born there.
（我的故鄉是新竹，我在那裡出生。）

B： Nantou is my hometown. I grew up in Nantou.
（南投是我的故鄉，我是在那成長的。）

5.**Q**： Which do you prefer, noodles or rice?
（麵或飯，你比較喜歡哪個？）

A： I prefer eating rice.
（我較喜歡吃飯。）

B： I would rather eat noodles than rice.
（我喜歡吃麵甚於吃飯。）

6.Q：**If you had one wish, what would it be?**
（假如你能許一個願望，你會許什麼願？）

A：**I would wish that I were the most beautiful woman in the world if I had one wish.**
（假如我能許一個願望，我希望我是世界最美的女人。）

B：**If I had one wish, I would wish that my parents were rich.**
（假如我能許一個願望，我希望我父母是有錢人。）

7.Q：**How do you feel about this test?**
（你覺得這次考試如何？）

A：**This test is difficult for me. Some of the questions are too hard to answer.**
（這次考試對我來說太難了，有些問題很難回答。）

B：**I think the test is easy, though I am a little nervous. I hope I can pass it.**
（我覺得這次考試很簡單，雖然我有點緊張，我希望我能通過。）

重點筆記

口說模擬試題第五回【試題】

請在十五秒內完成並唸出下列自我介紹的句子：

My test number is （初試准考證號碼） , and my seat number is （口試座位號碼） .

第一部份：複誦

　　共五題。題目不印在試卷上，經由耳機播出，每題播出兩次，兩次之間大約有一至二秒的間隔。聽完兩次後，請立即複誦一次。

第二部分：朗讀句子與短文

　　共有五個句子及一篇短文，請先利用一分鐘的時間閱讀試卷上的句子與短文，然後在一分鐘內以正常的速度，清楚正確的朗讀一遍。

> One: He is stuck at home with the flu.
>
> Two: I hope that it won' t trouble you too much.
>
> Three: The concert started at 7 p.m. and finished at 9:30 p.m.
>
> Four: We apologize for the inconvenience.
>
> Five: Let's take a walk to the train station.
>
> Six: Smoking is harmful to our health. It is not only harmful to smokers but also to people around the smoker. Some people have gotten lung cancer from

second-hand smoke. For your own health and the health of others, please do not smoke.

第三部份：回答問題

　　共七題。題目不印在試卷上，經由耳機播出，每題播出兩次，兩次之間約有一至二秒的間隔。聽完兩次後，請立即回答，每題回答時間為十五秒，請在作答時間內儘量的表達。

※請將下列自我介紹的句子再唸一遍，請開始：

My test number is 　(初試准考證號碼)　, and my seat number is (口試座位號碼)　.

口說模擬試題第五回【解答】

請在十五秒內完成並唸出下列自我介紹的句子：

My test number is ___711540___ , and my seat number is ___293686___ .

(虛擬初試准考證號碼)　　　　　　　　　　　　　　　　(虛擬口試座位號碼)

第一部份：複誦

　　共五題。題目不印在試卷上，經由耳機播出，每題播出兩次，兩次之間大約有一至二秒的間隔。聽完兩次後，請立即複誦一次。

1. Excuse me, sir!

（先生，抱歉！）

2. Hold on a moment.

（稍待片刻。）

3. Sorry, can you say that again?

（抱歉，你能再說一次嗎？）

4. I went to Kenting National Park last weekend.

（上週末我去墾丁國家公園。）

5. What a wonderful day!

（真是個美好的一天！）

第二部分：朗讀句子與短文

　　共有五個句子及一篇短文，請先利用一分鐘的時間閱讀試卷上的句子與短文，然後在一分鐘內以正常的速度，清楚正確的朗讀一遍。

One: He is stuck at home with the flu.

（他得了流行性感冒而正窩在家裡。）

Two: I hope that it won' t trouble you too much.

（我希望沒有麻煩到你。）

Three: The concert started at 7 p.m. and finished at 9:30 p.m.

（那場音樂會晚上七點開始，九點三十分結束。）

Four: We apologize for the inconvenience.

（我們對於造成的不便之處感到抱歉。）

Five: Let's take a walk to the train station.

（咱們散步到火車站吧。）

Six: Smoking is harmful to our health. It is not only harmful to smokers but also to people around the smoker. Some people have gotten lung cancer from second-hand smoke. For your own health and the health of others, please do not smoke.

（抽煙會傷害我們的健康，它不只傷害抽煙的人，也傷害抽煙者周遭的人。有些人因為二手煙而得到肺癌，為了你自己的健康及其他人的健康，請不要抽煙。）

第三部份：回答問題

共七題。題目不印在試卷上，經由耳機播出，每題播出兩次，兩次之間約有一至二秒的間隔。聽完兩次後，請立即回答，每題回答時間為十五秒，請在作答時間內儘量的表達。

1.Q：Do you like to study English? Why or why not?
（你喜歡學英文嗎？為什麼或為什麼不喜歡？）

A：I do not like to study English because it is so difficult.
（我不喜歡學英文，因為它很難。）

B：I like to study English because it is fun to learn another language.
（我喜歡學英文，因為學習另一種語言很有趣。）

2.Q：What can you do in the park?
（你可以在公園做什麼？）

A：I can hang out with my friends in the park.
（我可以跟朋友在公園閒逛。）

B：I can have a picnic in the park with my friends.
（我可以和朋友一起在公園野餐。）

3.Q：How long have you studied English?
（你英文學多久了？）

A：I've studied English for 5 years.
（我英文已經學五年了。）

B：I have studied English since I was a fourth grader.
（我從四年級就開始學英文了。）

4.Q：**What do you usually do on the computer?**

（你通常用電腦做什麼？）

A：**I usually chat with my friends on-line.**

（我通常在線上跟朋友聊天。）

B：**I usually play some exciting on-line games and sometimes do my homework on the computer.**

（我通常會玩一些刺激的線上遊戲，有時會用電腦作功課。）

5.Q：**Where can you see a lot of animals?**

（你可以在那裡看到許多動物？）

A：**I can see a lot of animals at the zoo.**

（我可以在動物園看到許多動物。）

B：**My grandpa's dairy farm has a lot of animals.**

（我爺爺的牧場有許多動物。）

6.Q：**Who calls you most?**

（誰最常打電話給你？）

A：**My best friend, Michelle calls me the most.**

（我最好的朋友，蜜雪兒最常打電話給我。）

B：**My boyfriend calls me at least twice a day. He calls me the most.**

（我男朋友每天至少打二次電話給我，他是最常打電話給我的人。）

7.Q ： **How did you come here today? How long did it take?**

（你今天是如何來這裡的？你花了多久時間？）

A ： **I took the bus. It took 30 minutes to get here.**

（我今天是坐公車來，到這裡花了三十分鐘。）

B ： **My father drove me here. It only took 10 minutes.**

（我父親開車載我來這裡，只花了十分鐘。）

必考單字附錄

- 天氣
- 人物
- 交通工具
- 節日
- 月份／日期
- 數字

與天氣有關的單字

hot	熱	dry	乾燥的
sunny	晴(天)	wet	濕的
warm	溫暖	humid	的
cool	涼	fog	霧
cold	寒冷	foggy	有霧的
rainy	下雨的	breeze	微風
cloudy	有雲的	typhoon	颱風
wind	風	snow	雪
windy	有風的	air	空氣

與人物相關的單字

parent	父母親	postman	郵差
grandparent	祖父母	police	警察
relative	親戚	scientist	科學家
cousin	表、堂兄弟姊妹	businessman	商人
nephew	外甥	cook	廚師
niece	外甥女	firefighter	救火消防員
doctor	醫生	waiter	服務生
dentist	牙醫	waitress	女服務生
teacher	老師	clerk	店員、收銀員
professor	教授	salesman	推銷員

與交通工具相關的單字

car	車子	vehicle	車輛、路上運輸工具
bus	公車	airplane	飛機
subway	地下鐵	jet	噴射機
bicycle =bike	腳踏車	helicopter	直昇機
scooter	小輪摩托車	ship	船、艦
motorcycle	摩托車	boat	小船

與節日相關的單字

New Year	新年	Mother's Day	母親節
Chinese New Year	農曆新年	Dragon Boat Festival	端午節
Lantern Festival	元宵節	Mid-Autumn Festival	中秋節
Valentine's Day	情人節	Moon Festival	中秋節
Easter	復活節	Thanksgiving	感恩節
April's Fool	愚人節	Christmas	聖誕節

月份的單字

January	一月	July	七月
February	二月	August	八月
March	三月	September	九月
April	四月	October	十月
May	五月	November	十一月
June	六月	December	十二月

日期的單字

first	一號	seventeenth	十七號
second	二號	eighteenth	十八號
third	三號	nineteenth	十九號
fourth	四號	twentieth	二十號
fifth	五號	twenty-first	二十一號
sixth	六號	twenty-second	二十二號
seventh	七號	twenty-third	二十三號
eighth	八號	twenty-fourth	二十四號
ninth	九號	twenty-fifth	二十五號
tenth	十號	twenty-sixth	二十六號
eleventh	十一號	twenty-seventh	二十七號
twelfth	十二號	twenty-eighth	二十八號
thirteenth	十三號	twenty-ninth	二十九號
fourteenth	十四號	thirtieth	三十號
fifteenth	十五號	thirty-first	三十一號
sixteenth	十六號		

Melody 老師的特別說明：

◎日期的說法是用序數的，例如：

5月1日 May first　5月2日 May second　5月3日 May third

數字的說法有二種，一種是基數，一種是序數。

● 基數是指像是：1、2、3、4、5、6、7、8、9、10…之類的
● 序數是指像是：第1、第2、第3、第4、第5、第6、第7、第8、第9、第10…之類的

1-20 數字的基數及序數

基數		序數	
1	one	第1	first
2	two	第2	second
3	three	第3	third
4	four	第4	forth
5	five	第5	fifth
6	six	第6	sixth
7	seven	第7	seventh
8	eight	第8	eighth
9	nine	第9	ninth
10	ten	第10	tenth
11	eleven	第11	eleventh
12	twelve	第12	twelfth
13	thirteen	第13	thirteenth
14	fourteen	第14	fourteenth
15	fifteen	第15	fifteenth
16	sixteen	第16	sixteenth
17	seventeen	第17	seventeenth
18	eighteen	第18	eighteenth
19	nineteen	第19	nineteenth
20	twenty	第20	twentieth

Melody 老師的特別說明：

◎ 發音： 在數字的說法上需注意發音相近的數字，像是 13/30，14/40，15/50，16/60，17/70，18/80，19/90 的讀音是不同的，需要特別注意。這些同時也是英檢口說命題者的最愛。

十位數

基數		序數	
10	ten	第10	tenth
20	twenty	第20	twentieth
30	thirty	第30	thirtieth
40	forty	第40	fortieth
50	fifty	第50	fiftieth
60	sixty	第60	sixtieth
70	seventy	第70	seventieth
80	eighty	第80	eightieth
90	ninety	第90	ninetieth

百位數及千位數以上的數字

百位數			
100	one hundred	600	six hundred
200	two hundred	700	seven hundred
300	three hundred	800	eight hundred
400	four hundred	900	nine hundred
500	five hundred		

千位數以上			
1000	one thousand	7000	seven thousand
2000	two thousand	8000	eight thousand
3000	three thousand	9000	nine thousand
4000	four thousand	10000	ten thousand
5000	five thousand	11000	eleven thousand
6000	six thousand	12000	twelve thousand

全民英檢解題攻略

　　曾利娟老師累積多年的教學經驗，加上赴美進修的心得，創造出獨特的圖像式單字記憶及圖像自然發音等法則。為了能夠幫助更多人，曾老師將各種背誦秘訣編輯成冊，毫不保留地公開所有技巧，讓同學們都能瞬間提昇英文能力。

　　只要記住曾老師所傳授的方法，不用死背，就能獲得英文大跳躍的武功秘笈！

圖像單字記憶法
定價250元

圖像自然發音法
定價180元

English Guide 102

全民英檢初級口說測驗（附1CD光碟）

著者	曾利娟（Melody）
責任編輯	劉宜珍
美術編排	賴怡君、黃寶慧
審校	Josh Myers、Andrew Walton
校稿	呂昱慧、葉勇成（Johnson Yeh）
錄音人員	Laura Titus Heffner、Melody 曾
錄音製作	佳信視聽傳播
內頁繪圖	徐世昇

發行人	陳銘民
發行所	晨星出版有限公司
	台中市 407 工業區 30 路 1 號
	TEL:(04)23595820　FAX:(04)23597123
	E-mail:morning@morningstar.com.tw
	http://www.morningstar.com.tw
	行政院新聞局局版台業字第 2500 號
法律顧問	甘龍強律師
印製	知文企業（股）公司　TEL:(04)23581803
初版	西元 2006 年 11 月 25 日

總經銷	知己圖書股份有限公司
	郵政劃撥：15060393
	〈台北公司〉台北市 106 羅斯福路二段 95 號 4F 之 3
	TEL:(02)23672044　FAX:(02)23635741
	〈台中公司〉台中市 407 工業區 30 路 1 號
	TEL:(04)23595819　FAX:(04)23597123

定價 250 元

（缺頁或破損的書，請寄回更換）

ISBN-13　978-986-177-050-5

ISBN-10　986-177-050-X

Published by Morning Star Publishing Inc.

Printed in Taiwan

國家圖書館出版品預行編目資料

全民英檢初級口說測驗／曾利娟著.－－初版.
－－臺中市：晨星，2006〔民95〕
136面； 22.5公分.－－（English Guide ； 102）

ISBN 978-986-177-050-5（平裝附1CD光碟片）

1.英國語言 - 問題集

805.189   95016510

407
台中市工業區30路1號

晨星出版有限公司

更方便的購書方式：

(1) 網站：http://www.morningstar.com.tw

(2) 郵政劃撥　帳號：15060393

　　　　戶名：知己圖書股份有限公司

　　請於通信欄中註明欲購買之書名及數量

(3) 電話訂購：如為大量團購可直接撥客服專線洽詢

◎ 如需詳細書目可上網查詢或來電索取。

◎ 客服專線：04-23595819#230　傳真：04-23597123

◎ 客戶信箱：service@morningstar.com.tw